ADULTERIES,
HOT TUBS &
SUCH LIKE
MATTERS

ADULTERIES, HOT TUBS & SUCH LIKE MATTERS

WILLIAM McCAULEY

THE PERMANENT PRESS
Sag Harbor, New York 11963

For information, address:
   The Permanent Press
   4170 Noyac Road
   Sag Harbor, NY 11963
   www.thepermanentpress.com

Library of Congress Cataloging-in-Publication Data

McCauley, William, 1937-
   Adulteries, hot tubs & such like matters / William McCauley.
      p.   cm.

   ISBN-13: 978-1-57962-154-4 (hardcover : alk. paper)
   ISBN-10: 1-57962-154-6 (hardcover : alk. paper)

   1. Couples—Fiction. 2. Married people—Fiction. 3. Humorous stories, American. I. Title.

PS3563.C33758A63 2007
813'.54—dc22   2007018616

Printed in the United States of America.

To Cheryl

CONTENTS

THE ARDENT ADMIRER

A cold wind gusted between buildings, swirling dust and litter into the air. The portly, overcoated man lowered his head and grabbed his hat. He continued against the wind to the intersection, where he stopped and waited. When the green light showed he joined a flow of pedestrians, mostly students, moving into the crosswalk. He walked briskly, for he had only twenty minutes to make his way across the upper campus to the faculty meeting. Nevertheless, he paused when he came to the flower shop on Campus Parkway, and looked through the window upon the familiar interior.

For years it had been his habit every couple of months to walk to the shop and select a bouquet of flowers to take home to Alice. It had started a few weeks after their marriage, as a declaration of love. Of course it was also a sort of insurance against the waning of love: a reminder to himself of how he had allowed carelessness to intrude, and, eventually, doom his first two marriages.

But over the decade of this marriage the spontaneity of the gift had become expectation of the gift, and then mere ritual. Gradually, the intervals between his floral offerings lengthened, which she did not seem to note; and when, finally, he stopped bringing flowers home, she did not seem to notice that, either.

When was the last time he'd visited the flower shop? This question made him a bit uncomfortable, but he was made even more uneasy by the stem of the question, for it seemed to perfectly encapsulate the state of their relationship: *When was the last time. . . ?* He impulsively pushed the door open, entered the shop, went to the big cooler door in the back, and looked through the glass at the display of flowers.

"May I help you?"

He turned to the young woman who had approached him. "The roses," he said, pointing. "The red ones in back."

The young woman entered the cooler and worked her way through the display of cut flowers to a vase on a pedestal, which she took up and then carried back through the display.

"Those will do very nicely. How many are there?"

She counted. "Fifteen."

"I'll take them."

She led the way back to the wrapping table. "Do you want them in a box?" she asked over her shoulder.

"A box *is* traditional, I suppose."

She smiled. "Nothing is traditional any more."

"I think long-stem roses should be in a box. Can you deliver them today?"

"If it's local."

"The University."

"Oh, sure, that's no problem. Do you want a card with it?" She pointed at a display at the end of the counter. He selected a card and passed it to her.

"She likes baby's breath."

"We nestle them in baby's breath and fern. I'll make a nice arrangement."

"You always do."

"And I remember you as well. You always selected such interesting combinations of flowers; so many colors."

He handed her a credit card. "If you have poor taste, choose gaudy."

"I always thought you had good taste. Selecting these proves it."

"For some reason I never chose roses. At least I don't remember choosing roses."

"Roses are predictable, and some say boring," she said. "Choose daisies and tulips when you like taking a risk. You probably like risking."

"Possibly," he said, pleased by her words. "Will you inscribe the card for me? My penmanship is terrible. Just write, 'For Alice, with love from Ben.'" He pulled his gloves on and watched as she wrote the words. And then he had a thought: "No, discard that. Write this instead: 'For a very lovely lady, from a very ardent admirer.'"

She got another card and wrote the words. "No name?" she asked, looking up.

"No, just what I said. It will make her remember something, and it will please her."

He left the flower shop feeling good about reviving his old gesture of love, and about echoing it with an expression that he had once used to characterize his feelings for her—she would understand that spontaneity and remember the phrase. She would like the surprise in it.

જ

He passed the rest of the day trapped in one ungratifying task after another: in mediating Larry Garson's dispute with Bill Meany about the latter's plan for offices in the new annex, which Garson characterized as "a fucking waste of money, for which I refuse to release one fucking dollar of my research budget"; and in defending his own Operating Budget draft, which was defeated by one vote; and, after the faculty meeting, in two lengthy thesis committee meetings, followed by a session with his most senior doctoral student, revising a research proposal the young man couldn't get right.

In none of these tasks did he take pleasure. In fact, he was aware even more acutely than his colleagues that his disinterest in these activities, which are the messy blood and guts of academic life, made him a mediocre department chairman, a leadership deficit that made his five-year tenure in that obligatory position much rougher and more unpleasant than it needed to be. Notwithstanding these annoying diversions, he left his office at five o'clock still as full of enthusiasm as when he had departed the flower shop—because he had made Alice's life, and thereby his own life, happier. Love does that.

∳

Ben had set the table, prepared a salad, gotten a fillet of salmon ready to poach, and had almost finished his second glass of wine when he heard the garage door open. He refilled his glass, poured hers, and carried both into the entry hall to greet her.

She kicked her shoes in the direction of the closet and approached him, still coated and clutching her briefcase, which, as usual, was crammed with papers and books. She leaned into his face and brushed his lips with hers, then turned away and dropped her burden at the base of the stairs before removing her coat and hanging it in the closet. She took the glass of wine he offered and sighed hugely, as if to demonstrate that now, finally, she was home and free of care.

"Bad day, my dear?" he asked.

She shrugged. "Not so bad, I guess, but tiring."

"You've the weekend to recover."

"I'm afraid not. The dean has identified still another problem with my proposal. He says the vision is still too ambitious. I think that when he whittles me down to three sentences in one paragraph with a budget of ten dollars he will think it just about right. So I brought it home." As one, they moved toward the kitchen. "But I expected that. What I didn't expect was the news that Caroline failed her comps again. She is thoroughly discouraged and ready to quit. She wants a meeting tomorrow to talk about what to do next."

He positioned himself on the business side of the island— his signal that she was off the cooking hook on this night. Her only duty was to draw up a stool, sit on the opposite side of the island, and simply watch. "One never knows about some students," he said, swirling the wine in his glass. "I think the comps don't mean much in her case, except to confirm that she's a lousy test-taker, which you've known all along. But I always thought she had the only important qualities: she's bright and damned good at getting things done."

"I know, dear. I'm way ahead of you. I'm not giving up on her. But the solution to the problem must wait until I get out of work uniform and into something comfortable. You're acting like you're the cook tonight."

"Yep."

"You're so wonderful."

"Shall I start the rice and the salmon, or do you want to drink several glasses of wine first?"

"I think several glasses of wine are more interesting than salmon right now—let's start there." Carrying her glass, she turned and entered the hall.

He heard the stairs creak. Though he was vaguely disappointed that she hadn't mentioned the flowers, his mild inebriation enabled a kind of lofty indifference. Perhaps they'd been delivered to the wrong building, or not at all. He would call the flower shop in the morning. Putting the roses out of his mind, he put water in a pot and placed it on the back burner, then topped his glass with wine and went through the hall into the library. There he sat and turned on a reading lamp and picked up the newspaper. He was browsing the sports page when she entered the room in a bathrobe, carrying her glass and the half bottle of wine. He looked up, noting that she'd scrubbed the makeup from her face; and that her hair clung wetly to her head, making her face seem wide and pale, and more than a little coarse in its revealed plainness, reminding him of his early-in-the-marriage discovery that she benefited more than most women from makeup.

"I took a shower, thinking we might want to do a tub before dinner."

"Of course," he said, with as much enthusiasm as he could manage. He did not enjoy the hot tub—for him the outcome was always enervation and a sleepy, unproductive evening. Early in their marriage—to please her, and, probably, to prove to her that he had the energy and adventurousness of her generation—he'd agreed to a remodeled deck and a new hot tub. He'd expected her enthusiasm would wane as the newness wore off. It hadn't. She became a devotee, and he, perforce, her less devoted tub partner.

In the hot tub she talked animatedly about the latest developments in her project, about her plan to convince Caroline that she should stay in the program until they could find a way to finesse the comprehensive exams, about the loveliness of the nearly full moon; and he, dulled by the hot water and four glasses of wine, wondered at, and envied, her energy and her almost manic cheeriness. He suffered the heat for ten minutes before mumbling something about getting dinner ready, and climbed out into the welcome cold. As he lumbered, naked, across the moonlit deck he felt conspicuous, fat, drunk, exhausted, and old.

❧

A woman's voice came on the line. "Campus Florist."

"This is Ben Kelleher. I bought some roses from you yesterday and asked for them to be delivered on campus."

"Yes, I remember."

"I'm wondering if they were delivered okay."

"I'm sure they were, or I'd have learned about it. But let me check with our delivery man."

He waited for a half minute, and then he heard her voice again. "Yes, at three-thirty. Alice Kelleher signed for them."

"Very good. Thank you."

He placed the handset on its cradle and went to the window. There he looked out at the great expanse of the quadrangle, which was quite colorless under a gray, wet sky. The branches of the Japanese cherry trees, which filled the grassy spaces between crisscrossing walkways, were bare and black. It was two-twenty, and the glistening walks were filling with students flowing out of the six buildings that surrounded the quad.

He wondered why she hadn't acknowledged the flowers, and why she had left them at her office. He told himself that she had probably just forgotten. It was the simplest explanation. But he had no time to think about it now; he had a two-thirty lecture and, following that, an hour and a half of office hours—with every time slot filled by a student ready to argue for a revised mid-term grade. Moreover, he reminded himself, she was as busy as he was, so it was understandable that she might forget to mention the flowers. He gathered together his umbrella, overcoat, and briefcase, and left the office. As he descended the stairs the thought crossed his mind that maybe she just didn't know he'd sent the flowers and was too embarrassed to mention them. This made him pause, because he realized that he had possibly created an uncomfortable situation for her, and, thereby, for himself when she found out *he* was the unknown admirer. If that was the case—that she thought some anonymous person sent the flowers—it was indeed a silly situation that he must put right immediately.

℘

There was voice mail from her when he got home. She'd called at five o'clock to tell him that she wouldn't be home until after eight. He drank a glass of wine while he cooked. After eating his omelet he poured a Grand Marnier, which he took to the library, where he read the newspaper. He cooked an omelet for her when she got home, and sat with her while she ate. He did not tell her that he had sent the flowers, in part because he wanted to give her a chance to acknowledge them, but also because it was certain to be an awkward moment if she did not know he'd sent them, and she would likely be embarrassed. So they talked for some time, over wine and cheese, about her proposal, the politics of his operating budget, and Caroline's unfortunate decision to quit the program and return to California.

When she sighed tiredly and said she had to work on her proposal for an hour before bedtime, he said, rather awkwardly, "Did you like the roses? Hadn't sent you flowers for a long time, so I thought—"

"It was *you?*" Her expression of disappointment, so nakedly truthful, silenced him.

ADULTERY

"Is it just my imagination?" Irma asked. She was leaning on the island counter, watching Marian sprinkle parsley over a plate spread with hummus.

"No, she *is* getting worse." Marian picked up a bottle, dribbled olive oil over the preparation, and pushed the plate across the counter toward Irma.

"She never stopped yakking all the time I was there," Irma said as she scooped a wedge of pita bread through the hummus.

"Her memory's gone," Winston said. "When she rambles like that she's really just fishing around for her topic. The last time we were there it struck me that one sentence almost never relates to the next. By the time she gets past the verb she's forgotten the subject, *and* the object, but she still feels she hasn't completed her thought—because she can't remember what went before. In effect, she's just saying whatever pops into her mind, trying to complete it."

Winston had just come up the stairs and was leaning against the wall beside the basement door. He smiled, sympathetically and a bit sadly, to show he wasn't being analytical, which he was, or mean-spirited, which he wasn't. In fact, he *was* saddened by Mom Kinchelo's rapid decline, because he genuinely liked her. She was the only member of Marian's family—other than Marian, of course—who didn't hate him. Irma, who hated him more than the others, glared at him.

Marian, in sisterly solidarity, gave him one of her tired *sweetheart, just shut up* looks. Then the sisters, as if on some timing internal only to them, instantly forgot he was there; they simply resumed their communication about Mom Kincheloe's disappearing cranial connections, while he quietly opened the basement door and slipped down the stairs into the basement where he resumed his communication with the plants about *their* affliction. He'd come upstairs only reluctantly anyway, to discharge his duty as host, an obligation that was satisfied by an appearance in the kitchen just long enough to irritate his sister-in-law.

Ten feet beyond the foot of the stairs two artificial suns blazed down upon a flock of young tomato starts, pots of head-high corn, trays of seedling annuals, and hydroponic troughs populated by clusters of parsley, basil, oregano, thyme, chervil, horehound, savory, tarragon, and other herbs. The lush nursery was enclosed by shimmering space blankets—plastic sheets with a metallic reflective surface that he'd suspended on wires to contain the energy of the twin halide suns. From one corner of the indoor garden a fan pushed a humid breeze through his miniature jungle.

He went around the nursery to the workbench and removed the magnifying glass from its position on a wall that was covered by tools hanging against matching white silhouettes. He opened a drawer and removed a foam-rubber kneeling pad, then drew aside one of the silvery space blankets and entered his nursery. He dropped the pad on the concrete floor in the narrow lane between troughs and lowered himself to his knees. Through the magnifying glass he inspected a leaf. That morning, during a routine inspection, he'd discovered tiny white dots on the same plant. A closer look through the glass had revealed a nascent infestation and he had occupied the better part of the next hour picking aphids with tweezers.

He knew how the insects had gotten in. Marian had once again used his outside tools inside or she'd worn her outside gardening clothes in the basement. "You spray, anyway," she always said, when he accused her. Which wasn't the point.

He heard the basement door open and the stairs squeaked heavily, followed by a deep, coarse voice: "Hey, man—you down there?"

"Yes." Winston turned, and, still kneeling, watched Norman pull a space blanket aside and enter the garden with a bottle of beer in one hand. Big-bellied, fat-faced, short-necked, he could have been mistaken for his sister Irma if he hadn't lost his bush of crinkly hair and she'd grown his coarse stubble of beard.

Contemptuous Norman, Spiteful Irma, and Angry Norbert: siblings that Mom Kincheloe had ejected from her belly to infest the world one morning forty-two years before. For years Winston had tried to gain their acceptance—even when they were teen-agers intent on destroying his blossoming romance with Marian. After nearly twenty-five years the only success he'd experienced was with Norman, whose contempt sometimes softened to amused tolerance when he needed something from Winston.

"I bought the light you said to buy, but they don't tell you how to hang it. I need to see how you did yours." Shading his eyes from the brilliance of the halide lamps, Norman squinted up at the floor joists, into which Winston had driven nails, from which simple monkey fists of twine suspended power cords.

"Guess I can manage that," he said. His gaze swept around Winston's nursery. "Still can't understand why you bother with this shit. You can buy it in any grocery store." He watched Winston study the leaf of a plant through his magnifying glass. "What're you doin'?"

"Removing aphids."

"Bugs?"

"Yes. Very tiny bugs."

"Yer pickin' *bugs* off those plants with *tweezers?*" One side of Norman's mouth curled in a contemptuous smile.

"Yes."

"Ever heard of bug spray?"

"Most of these plants are food."

"Don't you think the fuckin' food you buy in the grocery store has bug spray all over it? Shit's been *washed* in bug spray."

Winston crushed the tiny white dot of an aphid between the metal blades of his tweezers. Of course Norman was right about the spraying. And in fact he *would* spray, though not with the noxious potion Norman would doubtless deploy in his own nursery, if he ever got it going. When Winston sprayed, it was with a soapy mixture of his own formulation, which was safe enough to use in a baby's bath. But he would spray only after he'd picked by hand all the insects he could find by eye. He did not bother to explain to Norman the tactile satisfaction that he experienced from physically defending his plants, nor did he describe the esthetic pleasure he derived from seeing their lush green unsullied by black bug corpses or the gray residue of his soapy insecticide. These gratifications were too refined for Norman to comprehend.

Norman spoke. "I put them seeds between wet paper towels, like you said. Works fine. There's some already sprouted."

Winston turned a leaf to inspect its underside. Finding it clean, he looked at the underside of its neighbor.

"Gonna get the dirt and pots next. It's gonna get crowded, but what the fuck, all's I do is sleep there anyway. Since Sandee left." Silence for several seconds, then: "You know what the cunt had the balls to do? She calls me and tells me she wants that emerald ring I gave her for our first anniversary. I told her to fuck herself an' when she got through screamin' I told her I'd have a brown trout deliver it." Another pause, during which Norman's expression became reflective. "I gotta admit I miss her. She's not worth a fuck at anything but fucking, but at that she is *the* best. No question about it. I'd put her up against anyone. A man daydreams about havin' a woman who does the tricks she can do on a dick. But it's a two-edged sword. You know what I mean—you seen how she's always checkin' out the way a man wears his pants. Even a puke like you." Norman smiled his contemptuous smile. "A man's imagination works on him when he sees his woman sizin' up every male crotch in the room. Ever time she's outta yer sight you wonder if she's doin' one of her tricks on someone else's dick."

Winston always became uncomfortable when conversation became confessional. This was much, much too intimate. He pushed himself to his feet. "Dinner'll be ready soon. We ought to go upstairs and join the others."

Norman didn't move. "You know what the cunt had the balls to tell me when I told her I was going to flush her ring?"

Winston shook his head and began to edge around Norman, who stood in such a position that he all but blocked Winston's escape.

"She told me she sucked *you* off, then fucked you. Can you imagine that? Told me you bent her over and did her standing up under these here lights."

Winston paled.

"When that cunt gets mad she's got a filthy mouth. You should've heard the shit she told me about you."

"I—I—"

"What?"

"I—I—I—"

Norman studied Winston's ashen face, some four inches from his own, like a cop might study the face of one of his cringing suspects. His gaze never left Winston's face as he raised his bottle of beer, drank in deep rolling gulps, lowered the empty bottle, and belched humidly in Winston's face. "But I knew why she said those lies. She wanted to hurt me, man. That's the only reason she'd tell me she fucked a puke like you. Don't you think?"

"My god—" Winston breathed.

"Gotta be that. I hate to think what I'd do if I found out my brother-in-law's been fuckin' my wife."

Winston tried to breathe. "My god, what a—a terrible—"

"Yeah, terrible," Norman said, watching Winston edge around him and draw the space blanket aside. "What I couldn't figure out is how she knew you got this little dark spot right in the middle of the head of your dick. An' that your dick's on the small side. An' that it's bent a little to the left. All those *de*tails."

Winston stopped dead in his tracks, his hand outstretched with the magnifying glass just inches from its white silhouette.

"Is that right, man? What she told me—that you got this cute little liver spot right in the middle of the head of your dick?"

Winston heard a rustle of cloth against the space blankets, visualized Norman squaring around and unbuttoning his food-spotted sport jacket; visualized the way his food-spotted tie always hung under black-stubbled neck fat, the tie pulled open and positioned off to the left, as if in mockery of his, Winston's, left-tilted dick; visualized the movement of his right hand up to the armpit holster and the gleaming black steel of that little Glock 26. Winston's knees weakened and his bowels turned to water.

"That really bothered me, man. How could she *know* something like that? Then I understood. You know how women love to talk about their men's equipment? Well, Marian tells Irma, and that blabbermouth of course tells every fuckin' female in sight. I figure that's the only way Sandee could get to know your equipment. Don't you think?"

એ૭

"And when the bitch said, 'Oh, my, I can't buy this, it's got a little scratch in it,' I said, 'Well I'm not gonna *let* you buy it, lady, so why don't you stop bothering me and just fuck off.'"

Thus Norbert, eyes blazing and fat jowls ruddy with indignation, finished his story and crossed his arms. "I just wish I'd had the presence of mind to reach across the goddamned table and grab her by her fucking blue hair and drag her fat ass right out of the fucking store an' drop-kick it down the fucking mall."

They had just sung the happy birthday song to Norbert's wife, Susan, and while Marian cut the cake he had told the story about the blue-haired bitch who'd monopolized forty-five minutes of his time that afternoon with her stupid questions—stupid crap like "What's it made of? Does it have a guarantee? It's not going to fall apart, is it?"—crap he'd tolerated, as every salesman must. "Dumb bitch," he muttered, once again, just in case the others hadn't yet understood how aggrieved he was by the blue-haired old lady's behavior.

"You got a really dirty mouth," Norman observed. "You oughta listen to yourself sometime."

"Fuck you," said Norbert. "The cunt *was* a bitch—a dumb bitch."

Irma rolled her eyes over to the family arbiter and peace keeper, Marian. But she was busy dishing up a large ball of chocolate ice cream to accompany an equally large wedge of chocolate cake. This she passed to Norbert who, assessing its heft, decided it was sufficient and dropped it with a clunk in front of himself instead of passing it to his brother.

"How the hell do you think you're gonna sell your tables if you talk like that to your customers?" Norman asked, with a smile.

"She's not one of my fucking *customers*. That was the fucking point of the fucking story."

"Boys, boys," Marian said soothingly, referring to them in the collective diminutive form she'd used during their first twenty years, when they'd been at one another's throats more or less continuously. Marian had an air of moral authority that no one else in the family possessed—in part because of her ten-year seniority, but mostly because her lanky attractiveness contrasted so strikingly with their squat unattractiveness (*her* father was a tall, slim, slow-speaking, square-jawed, athletic Australian—a car salesman who had come into her mother's life only once, and then gone, all in the span of time required to buy a car from him and accept a load of his seed in the back seat of the same car; whereas, the father of the triplets was a long-haul truck driver, a squat fireplug of a man who had married and endured Mom Kincheloe just long enough to realize, after he helped her infest the world with the malignant triplets, that the four of them had him hopelessly outnumbered). "This is a birthday party, guys. Please let's keep it happy." She passed another plate of cake and ice cream to Norbert, who passed it to his brother. "Susan?"

Susan looked up from her plate, behind which she'd been making herself as small as possible, a basic tactic she'd long ago learned was prudent when her husband was looking for something or someone against which to unleash his fury. "It looks so nice," she whispered. "You did such a pretty job on the decoration—"

"Small piece, no ice cream," Norbert grunted through a mouth crammed with cake and ice cream. "She's on a diet."

"I'm really full, just a tiny piece for me," Susan whispered.

Like Susan, Winston sat quietly, hoping that silence and immobility would get him through the evening with minimum notice by, or contact with, his dinner guests. Earlier, he had broken his vow of silence by recklessly informing Norbert that he'd sent one of his friends to Norbert's table shop. Which was partly true. He'd suggested, offhandedly, to Jerry Neff, that before he bought that new kitchen table he'd been thinking about, he should see Norbert. Jerry had said, yeah sure, but of course never followed up on it. Of course Norbert, having taken the mention of a business referral as ironic, had reddened and snarled, "Fuck you." Winston had bitten his tongue and mentally berated himself for being so stupid. But during dinner his sympathy for Susan drew him out of his silence, and as Susan blew out the candles he'd carelessly offered a harmless remark to Norbert: "So how's business?" which he realized, as soon as the words escaped his lips, wasn't a harmless question. Everyone at the table knew that Norbert's business was always bad. Naturally, Norbert regarded Winston's comment as ridicule, which had sent him into his spittle-showering rage about the blue-haired old bitch who had objected to a minute, minuscule, almost microscopic scratch in the top of a birch table.

"Win, will you bring out the Reisling? And some clean glasses?"

Winston pushed his chair back and gratefully escaped to the kitchen. There he extended his few minutes of respite from the Kincheloe clan by leisurely clearing and then wiping down the cabinet top before getting the Reisling from the refrigerator, uncorking the bottle, and loading a tray with wine stems and bottle. Reluctant to return to the dining room, he'd let himself become lost in the clean-up chores of rinsing dishes and loading the dishwasher when he heard Marian calling him to bring the wine. Bracing himself to his duty, he assumed a butler's neutral demeanor and pushed through the swinging door into the dining room.

☙

Winston sawed the towel back and forth across his back. "They hate me. I don't know why you insist on my being here for these things. *They* don't want me here and *I* don't want me here. The only one who wants me here is you."

"They don't hate you," Marian responded from the bedroom. "It's true they resent you sometimes, but that's only when they think you're behaving like you're superior to them."

"I *am* superior to them. And so's everybody else in the world."

"See? There you go again."

Winston opened a cabinet door and dropped the towel down the laundry chute, then got a fresh towel and entered the shower enclosure and wiped it down. Finishing that, he dropped to his knees and worked his way over the tile floor, wiping up moisture. When he was sure he'd got it all, he dropped the second towel down the chute and walked, naked, into the bedroom where Marian had already climbed into their bed—encapsulated, he noted with disappointment, in her impenetrable flannel nightgown—and was in the act of fortifying herself further by pulling the comforter to her chin.

"They're a bit rough about the edges, but they're not so bad," she murmured.

One of Norman's jibes came to mind, and he looked down at his nakedness. "—a puke like you" was what Norman had said, with that glistening, fat-lipped smirk that had the effect of turning his lips disgustingly inside out. Well, this *you* wasn't such a bad-looking puke, all in all. A little skinny, Norman liked to note, with only a scanty half moon of hair on top and none at all on belly or chest, a fact the thoroughly-furred triplets liked to cite as evidence of arrested development, like, evidently, the size of Winston's equipment and its leftward wilt. He looked up at his wife.

"He spoke disparagingly about my equipment."

"He what?" she murmured.

"Norman said slanderous things about my equipment." He told her what Norman had told him earlier in the evening, in the basement.

"God! Norman can be the most dis*gust*ing creature."

In a voice that mimicked hers: "Oh-h-h, he's a little rough about the edges, but he's not so bad."

She turned onto her side to face away from him and said coldly: "Will you please turn off the light?"

"How did Sandee know about my little beauty mark? And my leftward tilt? And my supposedly inferior size? Which, when push comes to thrust, I don't agree is all that inferior. One would naturally assume the information had to come from you."

"It certainly did not!"

"How about your sister? You tell *her* everything. Bet you both get a lot of yuks about what you perceive as the inadequacy of my equipment."

"Winston!"

"Sandee had information about my equipment that could only come from you or my doctor. And my doctor is sworn to silence." He turned off the light and climbed into bed, bringing his knees up into the warm angle formed by the bend of her knees.

"Not so close. You're cold."

"The lamb was superb," he said, turning conciliatory now, because he wanted her. And, wanting her, knew he'd better say something nice about one of her siblings. He picked Irma. "Does Irma like her new job? Sounded like it's what she's been looking for."

"She already hates her boss. She's gonna quit again."

He draped his arm over her waist, felt his way under her arm to the ruffled bodice of her nightgown and cupped one of her breasts in his hand.

"Don't get any ideas."

"Just a quickie. You can relax and enjoy it—I'll do all the work." He felt for her nipple through the fabric.

"It's never just a quickie. I end up disrobed in a mess of blankets and sheets and I'm wet and sticky and wide awake and you fall sleep while I'm making the bed and cleaning myself in the bathroom."

"You won't even have to move. I can get it in from here. Just pull your legs up a little more." He brought his hand away from her breast and down over her hip and thigh until he found the hem, slipped his hand under it and up her leg.

She turned her face toward him. "Win—I had a day full of dreary meetings, followed by an exhausting evening of cooking and entertaining. All I need from you is silence. So I can sleep. Good night."

He took that as a *no* and drew away from her. Listening to her breathing smooth out into sleep, he let his mind slip into the reverie with which he had occupied himself during the dinner, in which Sandee, on her knees before him, her hands grasping his buttocks, her mouth enclosing his left-tilted equipment, sucked him off beneath the hot lights of his basement nursery. Minutes later, as the diminishing ripples of orgasm echoed pleasurably through his body, he tented the comforter high enough to keep it out of the warm puddle on his hairless belly and reached for a Kleenex.

❧

"Look, I don't want him wandering around my back yard smoking that stuff and leaving his paraphernalia all over the place," Winston said. He got up and brought the coffee pot to the kitchen table where he filled his cup, then Marian's. A few minutes earlier, while Marian prepared their omelets, he'd opened the back door and gone out on the deck. There, on the glass and metal table under the big umbrella, he'd found Norman's tiny brass pipe and a litter of spent matches.

"He was trying to be considerate," she said. "He knows we don't allow smoking in the house."

"Considerate? He was here for three hours, not three weeks. Not smoking his dope for the three hours he's here would be considerate. Doesn't he know who I work for?"

"You are such a control freak."

"Pot smoking is illegal. He, a former cop, would know that. I don't want him doing his illegal activities in my back yard. We have two paranoid neighbors and I have a damn good job that he puts in peril."

"Okay, okay, you made your point. You don't have to keep on about it."

"I've been making it for years."

"I said I'll tell him."

"I'm amazed he's still smoking that crap. He's bought that halide growing lamp and those seeds of his are sprouting. In six weeks he'll have a grow farm going in that kennel Sandee had the good sense to escape from. And then he'll be dealing."

❧

A cold residue of saag paneer, raita, rice, and lamb marsala had congealed in streaks and puddles on plates and in the take-out containers in which Marian had carried it home.

Beside an empty wine bottle was the bottle she had just opened. She filled her glass.

"Nathan called," she said.

He lowered the newspaper and looked at her over the top of his reading glasses. "Money?"

"He doesn't *al*ways call for money," Marian said. "For your information, he called to tell us he's found a job. An internship."

"He used the word *internship*?"

"No—he said—I don't remember, but it wasn't intern. What difference does it make?"

"The difference is this: an internship implies he's staying in school, a job implies he isn't. Did he say anything about school?"

"We didn't get into it."

"Who's it with?"

"I don't know—I didn't ask."

"What's he gonna be doing? Marketing? Sales?"

"We didn't talk about that."

"What *did* you talk about?"

"When I talk to Nathan I don't necessarily have the pecuniary motivation you have. I might want to know how he's *feeling*, for instance. Or how things are going with Sharon."

He waited for her to continue.

"He didn't *say* internship, but he did say something like that. I can't remember. We talked mainly about him and Sharon."

"Christ."

"He could do a lot worse than her, Winston."

"If he needed a wife. And I could afford to pay for one."

"They're all but married, anyhow. I don't know what difference it would make if they formalized it."

"Kids, that's the difference. Right now they're two single people who sleep together and fuck a lot. But being single, they are at least minimally influenced to reduce the risk of pregnancy. Get the picture? Being married eliminates that influence. You only have to listen to her for a couple of minutes to understand that she *really* wants kids. What's Nathan saying? He's not giving in, I hope."

"Why do you express their relationship so—in such pecuniary terms?"

"She's pregnant."

"She's not pregnant."

"How d'you know? Did you ask?"

"I did ask, but not for the reasons *you'd* ask."

He gave a short laugh. "My cretin sensibilities do not permit me to understand the distinction. However, I do know they've been living like a married couple for two years, which gives them the opportunity to fuck a couple of times a day. And I cringe with every fuck, because it is an opportunity for impregnation." He rattled the newspaper as he folded it. "Maybe I should send him a pile of money and a fistful of airline tickets. *I* think she'd be eating his dust in five minutes."

"You always undervalue relationships. And when you do, you undervalue people."

"When did we change the subject to me?"

Silence, tight lips, a touch of pink in her cheeks. He watched her fill her glass—for the fourth time, he noted. Or maybe the fifth.

"I think the clever little bastard is setting me up," he said, more maliciously than he meant.

"He's not a little bastard, he's our son."

"But he is clever. And manipulative. Even you have to admit that."

She glared at him, admitting nothing.

"We both know what's going on. First he softens me up with good news by letting me know he's got an internship—at least he *says* he's got one, whatever the fuck that means—to show me that he's serious about finishing school. Then he reveals the complication—that Sharon's pressing him for marriage, which he knows terrifies me—"

"Why can't you just believe what he says? Why do you have to think he's deceiving you?"

"—and then he innocently reveals that I can let him drown or save him—that is, I can abandon him to continuing in school and a situation which will—sooner rather than later, one gathers—lead to marriage with a brainless twit who will immediately begin popping out—"

"She is not brainless, she'll graduate with better grades than Nathan."

"—a brainless twit who will immediately begin popping out grandchildren whom I cannot afford to support—" he held up a finger to intercept her interruption "—*or* I can save him, and us, by giving him a pile of money and a handful of airline tickets and sending him off for the year of travel that he believes is his rightful rite of passage into adulthood."

"He's not capable of that kind of scheming."

Winston gave a brittle laugh. "He's been doing it all his life. He's so good at it he doesn't even know he's doing it."

෨

Winston cradled the pot between his stomach and his arms, the twin corn stalks rising above his neck and head. He struggled up the stairs, crossed the kitchen on the long banner of butcher paper he'd taped down to protect the hardwood floor, and went out the open doorway onto the deck. At the farthest corner of the deck, beyond the hot tub, he lowered the pot to a trivet. He went to the other side of the deck where he turned and looked back at the row of pots arrayed along the twenty-foot width of deck. Deep green leaves filled the space above the pots to a height of six feet. He went to the door, kicked off his shoes, and went inside and rolled up the butcher paper and put it in the recycling bin. After sweeping up a few stray particles of sand, he passed through the kitchen into the hall, a room-sized foyer that brought together kitchen, study, living room, and stairwell. He stopped at the base of the stairs.

"Marian! Come look at the corn."

She appeared at the top of the stairs in jeans and sweat shirt, brushing her hair. "I'll be down in a minute."

Winston went into the kitchen and turned on the espresso machine and got the grinder out of the cabinet. He was steaming the milk when she came into the kitchen. He led her out the back door, sweeping his arm out, as if introducing the plants.

"What d'you think?"

A reflective silence, then: "They're a bit assertive."

"Lush is the word you want. It's like you're at the edge of a jungle."

"Or a cornfield."

"You have no soul. Check it out from the patio table." He went to the table and sat. "C'mere, take a look."

She went to the patio table and pulled a chair out and sat, facing the hot tub and the wall of green. "It *is* cozy," she admitted. She glanced across the yard, then back to the wall of corn stalks, as if practicing the new coziness. "I do like the privacy."

"Mrs. Mackey's gonna be pissed."

She smiled up at him.

"Makes you want to strip right here and jump in the hot tub," he added hopefully. "We could do a tub right now."

A business-like shake of the head. "Much too much to do. Got a day full of errands. If I start the morning doing a tub I won't do anything else." She rose. "I'm going to the cleaners first. Are your shirts ready?"

"The sack's in the closet."

Winston watched her go inside. When she disappeared he rose and went to the edge of the patio and looked down the sloping lawn. Immediately below the patio was a rockery that was divided by two rectangular platforms, one situated below the other. He had built the platforms to serve as stairs and to provide a base for matching benches. The gardens of bedding flowers that he had planted over the course of the spring extended from a pair of grandfatherly rhododendrons that anchored each end of the patio. He considered the chores that he had planned for this day. He had already pruned the laurels along the back fence and moved the corn to the deck. All that remained was lawn mowing and aeration and uprooting the overgrown scotch heather above the rockery-bordered sidewalk in front of the house and replanting the area with moss pink and ice plant. It was time to deal with the heather, he decided, and headed for the tool shed.

∾

At eleven o'clock he stood, tired and sweaty, studying the sun-drenched rockery. He had uprooted heather plants and weeds, then turned the soil and raked it clean of stones and plant debris. Now the bed waited—smooth, loose, damp—to receive new plants. Clearing an area of garden that had grown tired and old, and planting springy starts of new color—it was this cycle of controlled renewal that drew him into his gardens, even in lifeless winter. Leaving the tools where they lay in the grass, he went across the yard to the garage and dropped the tailgate of the pickup and removed one of several flats of ice plants and moss pink.

When he finished the planting he hosed the sidewalk clean and set up a sprinkler, then carried shovel and rake and hand tools to the garage where he cleaned and dried them and then hung them at their assigned positions on the tool wall. He walked down the driveway and out into the circular cul-de-sac, into which his driveway and the driveways of the Mackeys, the Longstreets, and the Carlsons converged. In the middle he turned and studied the rockery. He decided it wanted more assertive flowering where the rockery and the driveway met. Gazanias came to mind. Spreading gazanias in white and yellow that would spill brilliantly over the gray face of the rockery.

He went inside and washed and went back to the driveway and backed the pickup down to the street. He drove along the stretch of park that half surrounded the four houses on his cul-de-sac, turned on Juanita Drive, and followed its curving ribbon of black down the hill through tunnels of alder and maple past intersections of streets that opened into clusters of houses—like the cul-de-sac in which he lived—which developers were gradually building over the fields and woods of Finn Hill. The road flattened at Juanita Beach, where he stopped at a crosswalk and waited for a man and a woman to herd a gaggle of children across the road. An oncoming RV slowed and stopped. When the children cleared the crosswalk he accelerated past the looming RV. Close behind the big vehicle was a topless red Miata, in which, as he passed, he glimpsed a pair of profiles: first a man's—sun-glassed, crew-cut, square-jawed, athletically thick-necked; then that of a woman with head thrown back in open-mouthed laughter—a woman who looked so astonishingly like Marian that— that—well shit, she had to *be* Marian. *Marian? In a red Miata*

with another man? Looking in the rearview mirror, he saw
the Miata make a right turn into a street lined by apartment
buildings. By the time he U-turned the pickup and raced to
the corner where the Miata had disappeared, all he saw before
him was an empty street lined with parked cars and rows of
three-tiered apartment buildings.

೪

Though he occupied the rest of the afternoon in his yard,
planting gazanias and weeding flower gardens and mowing
and aerating his lawns, his mind was not on his work. His
vividly-imagined images of Marian in the apartment of the
athletic driver of the Miata kept his insides churning and his
emotions bouncing. But even as his imagination gave sub-
stance to irrational suspicion he held doggedly to what his
rational side claimed was reality: that his tenth-of-a-second
glimpse of the woman in the red Miata was simply too brief
for him to certify her identify. A mere tenth of a second: *that*
was the reality. Still—the image that his retina had captured
was fixed in his brain as vividly as an image fixed on film, and
in such detail that the question was not whether the woman
in his head looked enough like Marian to be Marian (she did);
the question was whether his brain had fixed the image that
his retina captured or the image that jealousy fabricated.

An afternoon of hard work and a long, hot shower tem-
pered his imagination. By the time he'd wiped down the
shower and the tile floor, polished the steamed-up mirror,
replaced the almost-gone roll of toilet paper, brought out a
fresh stack of towels, and then dressed, the rational side of his
brain was winning the argument. His rational side convinced
him that even if Marian was the woman in the red Miata she

would have a simple and innocent explanation for her presence therein (with a sensually athletic man with whom she appeared to be having one hell of a good time).

 ℰ↻

"Me? In a red Miata?"

"Looked like you."

"Well, it wasn't me." Marian lifted the hinged barbecue cover and poked at the two steaks sizzling and popping above the gas flames. Smoke billowed out, rose, and drifted across the grass toward the fence that separated their yard from the Mackey's. She turned the steaks and closed the lid. Winston waited for her to continue. But she didn't; she lifted her wine glass from the barbecue tray, sipped, and returned to the table, which was set with plates and silverware.

"Near Juanita Beach," he prompted.

"I told you it wasn't me." She sipped her wine again and looked at the wall of corn stalks, then gazed out at the yard. "The yard looks very nice in this light. Even your cornfield. It's a perfect, private little park. And by the time the corn is finished, the days will be short enough that we won't need evening privacy. You do have a talent with plants."

"It's not talent. It's discipline. And planning."

"Whatever."

"All you need is desire. You have to want it enough to figure out how to do it. I didn't know a petunia from a rhododendron when we bought this place."

"I know, I know."

"Sure looked like you."

A smile of tolerant amusement—rather like the expression her Kincheloe siblings displayed when *they* regarded him—spread across her face. "What's with the cross-examination?"

Her smile destroyed his rationale for the investigation; and his suspicion now seemed as silly as high school jealousy. He saw that now it was he who was being examined. To wiggle out of the ridiculous position he made a stab at humor. "Thought you might be test-driving it. My birthday's coming up."

Still smiling that Kincheloe smile, she rose and went to the barbecue and raised the lid. She poked at the steaks with a fork as smoke billowed out. "They're done."

He went into the kitchen and got the salad from the refrigerator.

"Bring the wine!" she called.

The doorbell rang as he put the bowl and the bottle on the table. He looked at her.

"I cooked," she observed.

He rose and went back into the house and through the kitchen. Tall, patrician, imperious Martha Mackey was waiting on the front porch.

"I came to report another incident," she said.

"The kids again?"

She nodded. "It was definitely marijuana. I've smelled it too many times, coming from that patch of woods, to mistake it."

Winston nodded. "Well—if you're going to organize another meeting, let us know, we'll come." He edged back just enough to let her know, through body language, that he wanted to end the conversation.

"It was the evening you were entertaining over here. Family, I suppose."

"Yes. A birthday dinner. And speaking of dinner, mine's waiting for me right now."

"The odor was very strong and the wind was blowing it right across your backyard. I'm surprised you didn't notice."

"It was a cool evening. We were inside."

"Funny—I was sure some of you were out on the deck by the hot tub. Anyway, I just wanted to let you know I'm organizing another community meeting. This time I'm inviting the people who live on the other side of the park, by the school. It's *their* kids that are causing this problem. Maybe that'll get the police involved."

"Right. Just let me know when and where and we'll be there."

"I will."

He smiled. "I think I hear my steak sizzling at me."

"I'll let you know. I noticed you planted some corn on your deck."

"Yeah. Marian's idea. Hot tub privacy."

"Um."

"Thanks for organizing a meeting. Be sure to let me know when."

He watched her retreat down the stairs, waved when she glanced back, then closed the door and returned through the kitchen to the deck. Marian, refilling her wine glass, looked up.

"Mrs. Mackey," he said as he resumed his seat. "Invited us to another neighborhood war on drugs. Seems she smelled Norman's pot."

Marian rolled her eyes.

"You really must tell him," Winston added.

"I will, I will."

He cut into his steak, stuck a piece in his mouth, and frowned as he chewed. He swallowed, put the fork and knife on the table. "It's cold."

"Want me to put it back on the grill for a minute?"

"Please."

He offered his plate as she rose, watched her place the steak on the grill and close the lid. And he continued watching her as she sipped her wine and watched the steak through the glass in the lid.

❧

Winston retracted his leg from the hot tub and went to his knees on the deck. He opened the access panel and saw that Marian had turned it up again. She claimed that a hot tub, like a sauna, was therapeutic only if it was as hot as you could stand. Otherwise, why bother? If it was as cool as a bath, it *was* a bath, and bathing was a hygienic procedure that one performed in private, not in a social setting. Winston turned the heat control back, but of course hours would pass before the water temperature returned to the level he preferred. He stood naked and indecisive in the cool air of early June, feeling his skin tighten with the chill, looking down at the steaming water, wondering if it was feasible to run the garden hose into it for a couple of minutes. He decided that was too involved. Moreover, his sore body could probably benefit from a *hot* hot tub. Sitting on the edge, he swung his legs inside, submerging them one at a time up to his calves. The heat was intense. When the water covered his knees he paused for another minute, then pushed off and stood thigh deep in the hot water. Tendrils of steam rose about him. Now sweating, he lowered himself slowly—reflexively sucking his breath when the water's heat enclosed his genitals—until he was in a sitting position with the water at his shoulders.

He put his head back and allowed his body to slide forward until the water touched his chin. Sweat ran down his face. He gazed up into the night sky, which, being clear and moonless, should have displayed billions of stars against a velvet blackness—but sadly, didn't. The yellow-gray sky was dotted with a few lonely white specks that possessed enough brightness to show up against the perpetual blanket of urban light pollution—which, his theory held, completed urban mankind's disconnection from nature. He lowered his gaze to the wall of corn plants that was, at that very moment, frustrating Martha Mackey's curiosity and inciting her suspicion, which led his thoughts naturally to Norman and his pot, and to Norman's revelation of Sandee's shocking lie. My god, what kind of woman would make up a lie like that? Sandee's kind, apparently. But what, exactly, was her kind? What was she really like? He could not remember ever having had a thought about her beyond a first impression of homely empty-headedness. Until Norman related her lie, he, Winston, had scarcely noticed her. Still less had he regarded her as sexually attractive. An interesting insight into himself, he thought, smiling up at the polluted sky, conscious now of the sexually pleasurable combination of the water's heat and thoughts of Sandee. Yes, he admitted it: her lie had made her interesting. Any woman who would tell her husband that Winston had bent her over and did her with his left-tilted, beauty-marked equipment (after a blow job performed on that same equipment) in his basement garden was automatically interesting—even if it was a lie. And she was particularly interesting at that moment, because he'd not had sex with anyone, not even his wife, for over a month. He thought, momentarily, about marching into the living room and waking Marian from her stupor and demanding his right as a husband. But the thought passed. He didn't want groggy, sleepy Marian. He wanted the excitement of discovery, of newness, of wanton youth; he wanted Sandee. He pulled himself up on the edge of the tub and, steaming in the cool evening air, did himself.

TRADITION

"**I** don't practice criminal law, Marty."

"Okay. Then who?"

"I think Jack Callaghan. I'll call him and tell him you're a friend of mine. Tell me how it happened"

"There was no knock, no warrant, just busted the door off the hinges. They used a *battering* ram. Like we're a couple of armed criminals. There was this huge crash, yelling and screaming, and then all these guys in blue jump suits and flack jackets and machine guns. It was a quiet evening and we were getting ready for a tub and then the street was jammed with police cars—and the *noise!* Christ, the noise. It was terrifying. The house is a wreck—we got a sheet of plywood over the front door opening. We paid seven grand for that door, which is now a pile of kindling, and the Persian rugs're trashed, and the walls—"

"What'd they get?"

Marty looked at Garrison for several seconds. "Few ounces of pot. And some plants."

"You been *growing*?"

"It's not a big deal. Lot of people grow their own pot."

"It might be a big deal. How many plants?"

The significant question; Marty didn't need a lawyer to tell him that. "They were all starts," he said, as if to deflect the question.

"How many?"

Another silence. Then: "Forty."

Garrison's eye brows went up.

"I always did it that way, Garrison—I'd take three or four dozen cuttings and start them. After a couple of weeks you see which ones are viable, and cull them. The cops came before I culled. In a couple days I'd've had it down to four plants."

"You need to talk to Callaghan."

"Okay."

"How's June?"

"She was terrified—and weirded out. Utterly. This really did something to her, Garrison. I've never seen her so—distracted is the only word I have for it. We got bail about eighteen hours after they busted us, and she's still like a zombie. I think maybe she's coming out of it a bit now, but she's still scared to death. She wouldn't come down here to see you. No way. They handled her—very roughly. It was awful. We'd smoked a bowl and she'd gone to the bedroom to take off her clothes—we were going to do a tub. She was in the front hall right when the door exploded and these kids in flack jackets came charging in waving machine guns—*machine* guns, for God's sake. She screamed and ran for the stairs, where they grabbed her, buck naked."

"What about you? They do anything to you?"

"If a fat lip and a sore ear and a splitting headache and bruised ribs is okay, then I'm okay. This one guy, a kid, by the look of him, seemed very, very excited—he smacked me a couple of times before another cop pulled him off. The house is a mess, Garrison. You can't imagine. Looks like a war zone. Broken dishes and pots and pans and cereal boxes and sugar and flour all over the kitchen, beds upside down, clothes and books everywhere, drawers pulled out and dumped, broken glass."

"I'll call Callaghan, get you set up."

"Okay."

"And Marty—have you been giving pot to anyone?"

"I haven't been dealing, if that's what you mean."

"What did you tell the cops?"

"I don't really remember. I was panicked—but I think all I said was one thing, which I said several times, that it was my private stash."

"Did they get your address book?"

"Yeah. And my diaries, and my computer."

"Your diaries."

"Yeah. I've kept a diary since I was in high school. Not very interesting stuff."

"Anything, anything at all that can be construed as the records of a grow farm?"

"Just routine notes about which soil to use, what kind of lamps to buy, how much each plant produced."

Garrison leaned forward, his forearms on his desk, and spoke carefully. "This is off the record, Winston, because I'm a lawyer, and on this one you're not my client, and so what I'm gonna tell you could be construed as obstruction. But I am also your friend, so I'm going to tell you, anyway. You understand?"

"Yes, of course."

"They're gonna contact every name they can find in your stuff, and they're gonna say you named *them* as buyers and users. This is to characterize you as a dealer. And they're gonna contact neighbors and business associates."

Silence.

"You see how it works? I'm in your address book, so they'll come to me and tell me they nailed you, and that you named *me* as a buyer. They'll say they're going to prosecute me, but will offer to let me off if I cooperate. Of course this is simple fishing, but it's also the first step in manufacturing evidence. Even your good friends, and people who know nothing about your little grow farm—"

"It's not a grow farm."

"—will panic. The main problem for you is this: they might manage to get a couple of people to panic and to lie for them. If they sign a paper swearing you and June sold them pot—well, you see where this goes." He paused to let his words sink in. Then he added, "How many people know, actually *know* you grow, or have seen your little grow farm?"

"It's not a grow farm. And the only people who have ever seen it are a couple of our oldest friends. A few others know, and these are the ones we give some pot to from time to time."

"No one else?"

"No—unless one of them has talked about it."

"Yeah."

"And it appears that one of them has a big mouth. So here's the free advice I never gave you—you need to get on the telephone and tell those friends who have direct knowledge of your little growing operation what happened: that you've been busted, and that you have not implicated anyone. Tell them the cops got your address book and to expect a call. Tell that that the cops will lie and say you fingered them. Tell 'em you did not tell the cops anything. Tell 'em to get rid of their stash—if they've got one—and simply say they know nothing. All those folks will be all right if they don't panic. And remember: I never talked to you about this. Marty, do you think someone deliberately turned you?"

"I can't imagine who would."

❧

"Firearms in the house?" Callaghan asked. He was looking down at a yellow legal-sized note pad, scribbling.

"No," Marty said.

"You sure? A hunting rifle, a shotgun?"

"A pellet gun. For the squirrels."

"And you never been busted before?"

"I already told you. Not even a traffic ticket."

Callaghan stared at the yellow pad, which was densely covered by a scrawl of text. He looked up at Marty, and shrugged. "Of course, those starts really complicate things. But the good part is you're pretty much an ideal client to defend. The number of plants will make it hard to get you off completely. You could be looking at thirty days, maybe sixty. Suspended maybe, or work release."

"The cop said ten years."

"They like their customers to be afraid. Now, if they'd found a gun or you had a record, or if you were a black dude with no visible source of income, you'd be up to your eyeballs in trouble. But you're white and middle class; a guy with a good job; the rules are different for people like you."

"What about June? She's pretty beat up, mentally. I need to keep her out of this as much as possible. Can they touch her?"

Callaghan shook his head. "Nah. Not unless someone can finger her as a supplier—anyone actually *buy* from her or see her sell to someone? Or literally hand the stuff over?"

"I told you we never sold the stuff."

"Whatever. If all they got on her is she knew you were growing it, they got nothing. Knowledge isn't a crime. My guess is they'll leave her alone, unless they want your house. We haven't talked about that yet, and I guess we ought to now. The main thing is that if they want it, they'll have to find some evidence to show her as a party to your crime, because she's half owner. What's your equity?"

"We own it."

"You *own* your house?"

"Yes."

"What's it worth?"

"Seven-fifty, probably."

"How long you owned it?"

"We bought it nine years ago, and paid the mortgage off last year."

"You paid off a mortgage for seven-fifty in nine years?"

"We didn't *pay* seven-fifty for it," Marty said. "We paid three-twenty for it, but real estate appreciation and remodeling have increased its value."

"Where'd you get the money to pay it off? Can you verify a legitimate source?"

"I exercised some stock options. I was in a start-up that did okay."

Callaghan looked down at his notes, wrote a couple of lines, and looked up. "You need to understand that when the cops find out you own your house they will first assume you paid it off with ill-gotten gains, and will try to prove it. I assume we can show you got the money from stock options. That right?"

"Absolutely."

"Okay, the second thing that will happen is that they will almost certainly redefine your case. You will still be a criminal, of course, but you will also be a profit center." He paused for a few seconds, to let Marty figure out what he meant. "Seven hundred and fifty thousand bucks pays some police salaries and buys some nice gadgets that cops like to have. They have every incentive to make your small case into a big case. You need to get ready to have your little grow farm characterized as agribusiness."

"It wasn't a grow farm, or agribusiness."

"Whatever."

"Can we sell the house?"

Callaghan shrugged. "You might get away with it—if you can come up with a cash buyer today and close tomorrow. But I can't *tell* you to do anything like that. Let me put it this way: if you do it, you'll have to do it before they find out how much equity you have. And they will find out, if they haven't already, because they always check for equity."

"Shit."

Callaghan's lips moved into what Marty thought might be a smile. "It could be bad, if the cops do their job; but it might not be, because cops and prosecutors are also part of a big bureaucracy, and bureaucracies sometimes let stuff fall through the cracks."

"Is that the reason they're watching the house? That they know our equity?"

"What do you mean?"

"There's three of 'em. One's in a Porsche, one's in a fancy yellow van with big tires, and one drives a red Mercedes convertible."

"Three? You sure they're cops?"

"They come in a regular pattern. The Porsche comes down the street, slows at the house, turns the corner, parks for an hour maybe, then leaves; then a while later the van drives by and parks. Then it's the Mercedes. It's like that all day. Is that normal?"

"No. But I don't understand why they'd be watching you. Surveillance is expensive. Unless they're getting something out of watching you, they won't do it. They may be trying to get something that can make their case stronger. Well—you don't have to talk to them, and they can't come on your property without a warrant. If they come to you, ask for a warrant." Callaghan looked at his watch. "I got to be in court in a few minutes, so we gotta continue this later."

Marty rose and accepted the business card that Callaghan offered.

"Read the back," Callaghan said. He came around his desk and ushered Marty to the outer office and out into the long, empty, black-and-white-marble hall.

On the street Marty started his car, and he sat and read the tiny print on the inside of Callaghan's folded card:

Twelve ways to stay out of the slammer:
1. Avoid contact with alleged victims or state's witnesses.
2. Avoid contact with your own witnesses, unless directed to by your attorney.
3. If chemical dependency treatment is in order, start it now while you have choices.
4. Stay away from known criminals.
5. Do not drink and drive.
6. If you do not have a job, get a job. Any job.
7. Always be early for court.
8. Assume you are being watched.
9. Clear up all outstanding legal matters, whether they are warrants or parking tickets.
10. Clean your house, inside and out. Make it neat.
11. Get your driver's license, auto registration, and mandatory insurance up to date.
12. Clean your car inside and out. Check for everything, from contraband to defective brake lights and turn signals.

☙

How to account for denial on such a calamitous scale? Marty and June weren't stupid people, as most criminals are. They knew the rules: if the cops bust you with five or more plants the law presumes you're growing with intent to sell.

That's a critical distinction, one that every grower understands, because it's where the level of risk changes greatly. In fact, he and June talked about it often, though their conversations about risk usually took place when they were stoned and steaming in the tub, and therefore had a theoretical and a not-quite-real quality. They believed they had finessed the issue by only growing four plants in each crop cycle. Moreover, Marty had developed other measures to mitigate risk. To control physical exposure, he had installed exhaust fans that sucked the skunky basement air up through three floors to a vent in the roof. And of course he never sold pot to anyone. Nor did he give it to anyone, except the half-dozen couples who had formed the core circle of their close friends for all of the two decades since their college years.

They'd even talked about giving up pot, like they gave up other unhealthy behaviors such as cigarettes, fried foods, and saturated fats. June said no way. She wasn't any more likely to give up pot than she'd give up their sex toys.

So no decision became their decision. The weeks became months, the months years, and Marty's new consulting business with Jerry prospered. When the time came for cloning the next generation of pot, they'd do a pipe and then go downstairs and study the four lush and nearly mature plants, and take a dozen cuttings from each. A week or two thereafter he would select four of the most viable plants that took root, and uproot the others. A few months later he would stand at the basement workbench scissoring buds from dried and brittle twigs, his hands sticky with resin and the basement air redolent with the raw skunkiness of dried maryjane. In that environment, surrounded by filled baggies, he would recognize again the fullness of risk and he and June would talk about it again. They would vaguely reassure each other that, yes, it *was* time to cut back. The next crop would be one plant, they'd say, just for their own use. But it was as impossible to stop producing pot for their special friends as it was to stop producing pot for themselves. So it continued for year after year, with Marty and June sharing the abundant happiness produced by the best four plants of every growing cycle. In quarterly gifts they delivered little baggies of marijuana buds so potently encrusted with resin that they appeared to be candied.

Every one of the plants had descended from a single mother plant, a six-inch start given him by that stoned artist he'd befriended at the Blue Moon in the years when he was studying mathematics and June was a grad student in engineering. That was ninety generations ago. There was tradition here. Ninety generations of tradition. It was not such an easy decision to make, this decision to stop growing pot.

◌

"Jerry, they can't touch you."

"Can't touch me? We're partners—remember? Jesus Christ, what *possessed* you?"

"Jerry, you don't have to worry—"

"My business partner turns out to be a fucking drug linchpin, and I'm not to worry. Mary'll feel a lot better knowing I don't have to worry, particularly because the cop told *her* I was involved in some big-time growing operation with you, and that they were gonna seize the business and the house and throw both of us in jail if she didn't talk. And what *about* the business? I suppose now I have to get a fucking three-hundred-dollar-an-hour attorney to defend myself."

"Callaghan says they can't touch you or the business. And the cops lie about this kind of thing routinely, to spook you—"

"Yeah, well, I am spooked."

"They're fishing, they're trying to scare—"

"Fishing! Jesus Christ on a crutch!" He was yelling again. "My business is in danger here—"

"Jerry, calm down. You're gonna have another heart attack."

"Calm down?" He was screaming now. "Calm down? He turns my business into a fucking front for his fucking drug operation and drags my name in shit and I'm supposed to fucking *calm down*? I'm on the goddamned motherfucking *school* board, Marty!"

Marty heard a clatter against a background of Saturday morning TV, then wailing.

"Jerry? Are you there?" More clatter, a woman screaming, "Jerry!" Yelling, dishes breaking. "Jerry! Are you there? You okay?"

Mary's voice came on the telephone. "He gagged on something and vomited, but he's okay. I gotta hang up now and clean up this mess. Marty—I just can't believe you did this to us."

Marty felt a hand on his shoulder.

He looked up at June as he placed the handset on the cradle. "Jerry's pissed. So's Mary."

℘

"Losing the MarkWare deal, and then Jerry yelling at me again—that was when it happened. I lost it, came unglued. We were toe to toe, screaming at each other like two kids on a playground. Wilson separated us, but not before I told Jerry I damn well wasn't going to just walk out, that if he couldn't come up with the money to buy me out he'd just have to learn to live with a drug *linchpin* as his partner. I thought he was going to kill me, but he just threw a chair across the room and stormed out. He wasn't even out the front door before that airhead niece of his came into my office and whispered will I sell her some pot. That was my day. How was yours?"

June put her arm round his waist and pulled up against him. They stood on the deck that surrounded the hot tub, looking out over the long yard that dipped down to the creek. The shape and size of the backyard—it was over an acre of gardens and lawns, all well manicured—made it the most distinctive part of the property. They had recognized the uniqueness of the property the first time they saw it, though much of it was hidden beneath mountainous blackberry thickets. The house was eighty years old, the last remnant of a dismembered farm, around which a suburban community had gradually evolved.

Then the house had a tiny kitchen with worn-through linoleum and broken cabinets, small bathrooms with noisy, leaky plumbing, bedrooms and halls with gouged hardwood floors and peeling wallpaper, dangerous wiring, doors that stuck. But none of that mattered: the house's problems could be fixed with money, or a bulldozer. It was the position of the house on a little knoll, at the front of an acre and a half, giving it a magnificent view of the Cascades to the east, and an isolation imposed by a meander of creek and a greenbelt that gave it uniqueness. They bought the house without even seeing the upstairs.

"Mine?" she said lazily, her head against his chest. "Not bad, I guess. The only notable event of the morning was when Wagner called me into his office and canned me. 'Perhaps it would be better for all concerned if you resigned,' is what he *actually* said. I didn't agree to resign, so he had to can me. I was humiliated. I tried not to be, but couldn't help it. And I couldn't help just standing there and crying. I wish I hadn't."

They had been expecting this. Her position was too visible, too sensitive. He wrapped his arms round her.

"That was *my* day," she murmured into his chest.

"I hope you told him—" he was looking for something flippant, something outrageously irreverent, something that would tell her she did not have to care, that it didn't matter, that it was nothing. Something to make her laugh instead of cry. But every word he thought of speaking seemed far too hurtful to speak aloud.

A sniffle against his shirt. "I wish I hadn't cried." Another sniffle. "I boxed my stuff and Ron carried it out to the car for me. Marsha and Ron wanted to take me to lunch, but I said some other time. They were nice; they made me feel like I, we, didn't really do anything—"

He held her for another minute, felt her stir against his chest, and loosened his arms so she could draw away.

"I came home before noon, but I couldn't stay in the house. They kept driving by. I hoped Janice was home and she was, so I went over there. What do they want from us? Didn't they do enough already?"

"We have to be steady," he said gently. "They're trying to rattle us—and the neighbors. They're trying to scare the whole neighborhood. It's how they keep us off balance."

"Janice and Max feel it, too."

"You need a glass of wine."

"They're so supportive. It's amazing; they're not even our friends. When I was in the living room with Janice I realized I'd never been there before, and yet I sat there and watched the cops go by and we talked—very openly—about all of this shit, until her kids came home from school. I couldn't help feeling like a *crim*inal, like I'd done something shameful and deserved to get fired, but Janice defended us and said the cops were wrong, that they were—"

"I'll open a bottle of that Ashland Pinot. Then we can do a tub."

"Don't you feel it, Marty?"

"No."

"You don't feel—ashamed."

"No, of course not. What's to feel ashamed of?"

She didn't say anything.

"Listen, sweetheart. Don't let them do this. Don't let them make you feel ashamed. We didn't steal anyone's property. We didn't beat anybody up, or shoot anyone, and we haven't been supporting some drug-dealing pimp. We pay our taxes, we vote, we support charities. We've been doing something that's as private as sex, which harms no one. Because *they* think it's shameful doesn't make it shameful."

"I tell myself that, all the time, but it doesn't work. I can't be philosophical about it, like you. I don't even like our house anymore. When I came back today I didn't want to come inside. I sat in the car, wondering where I should go. Without you here, it was a hostile place. When they started driving by again I knew I don't want to live here any more. That's what I was thinking, that I don't want to live here any more. They've done something very bad to our house. Even to the neighborhood. It feels so threatening." She gestured at the long back yard. "Even this feels threatening."

He kissed her forehead, drew back, and went inside. He got a bottle from the cooler, opened it and poured two glasses of wine, returned with the glasses and a tiny metal pipe and a lighter, which he put on the bench. He went to the hot tub, folded the cover off, came back, and began unbuttoning his shirt. She watched him, her arms crossed over her chest, as he dropped his shirt on the deck, kicked his shoes to the side, pushed his pants and shorts off. He picked up the pipe, lit it. His belly was a small roundness, a tight ball of pink above a pubic patch of curly black hair.

"You trying to cheer me up?" she asked, smiling.

He nodded and handed the pipe to her, then began to unfasten her skirt as she drew on the pipe. "They can drive their Porsches by our house all they want," he said, "but right here we can do anything *we* want. This thing—how the hell do you get it loose? This is dangerous—what if your skirt got on fire and you had to get out of it quick?"

"Like now?"

"Like now."

"I guess I wouldn't have you do it."

She drew on the pipe, handed it to him, and released the clasp. The skirt dropped in a pile at her feet. He pushed her panties down, then removed her bra and kissed her. When a car went by on the street in front of the house she stiffened and listened.

"They can't come in here, they have to have a warrant," he murmured.

"They got one before."

"C'mon," he said, taking her arm. "There's one place where we're completely immune from them. Once we're in the tub they can't touch us, even if they have a warrant. It's the law."

She smiled. "I think you're bullshitting me."

"Swear to God. Callaghan told me."

❧

Marty and June had met Carol and Charlie a few times at the mailboxes or on neighborhood strolls, and they knew nothing more about them than their names, that Charlie was a stock broker, and that they had two young sons. Now they were at the front door, offering Marty their support and their sympathy.

Marty uneasily thanked them and asked them in, then called to June, who appeared from the kitchen.

Carol, who, though still in her early thirties had already taken on a matronly plumpness, smiled in commiseration and went to June and took her in her arms and hugged her. With some embarrassment, June allowed this intimacy, but drew back when Carroll released her, and gestured toward the kitchen. Murmuring welcoming phrases, Marty ushered them to the big round table that was the social center of their house. They talked about the shocking behavior of the police, avoiding direct mention of marijuana. Carol's gaze wandered about the kitchen, taking in the big gas range with its six burners, the glass-paned cabinet doors that revealed dishes, spices, and food; the hardwood floor; the herbs growing in a rack of pots and trays under the skylight.

"We all got together last night and talked about it," Charlie said. "Everybody on the block came. I told them what our lawyer told us, that we shouldn't say a thing to the cops without talking to him first. We could say we didn't know anything. But nothing more. And that's what I told that cop—the snotty young one who's been driving around the neighborhood. He even said he was going to Charlie's boss if we didn't cooperate."

"It seems to be standard operating procedure," Marty said carefully. "They like to make people fearful, to get them to cooperate."

"He talked to Charlie like he knew Charlie was concealing information from them," Carol said. "They won't get *me* to lie about anyone."

Charlie had been sitting solemnly with his arms crossed. Now he spoke up. "Mind you, we're not exactly *happy* about the situation. Living here for a year with a pot farm next door—and I never even got a toke. Not one." He gave a bluff laugh.

Marty slid a quick glance at June and saw that she had lowered her eyes.

"Did they get it all?" Carol asked innocently.

Marty did not like the drift of the conversation. "Our lawyer told us we shouldn't talk about it," he murmured.

"We haven't had any pot since we moved to Seattle," Charlie said. "We had all we wanted in Wichita, but we haven't made a good contact here. It's so risky going to the U District or Pioneer Square and trying to score. With a job like mine, one bust and I am history. So we haven't done a joint for over a year."

"Well—see, the thing is, our lawyer says we are not to talk—"

"They didn't *really* get it all, did they?" Carol said with a sly smile.

"Our lawyer—" Marty said

"In Wichita we had friends we'd gone to high school with, and then college, and half of 'em still smoke pot, so getting good weed was routine. But like I said, my freakin' job is so sensitive. One bust and I'm on the street. I been thinking about going up to Vancouver for a couple of days. Maybe get a six-month supply. But then there's the risk of getting it through the border."

Marty glanced at June, who was still looking down.

"I grew pot when I was at Wichita State, but no way I can do it now."

"I suppose," Marty said.

The doorbell rang. Marty rose and went to the living room and opened the front door. One of the cops who'd broken down their door stood before him, a sheaf of papers in his hand. Now he was dressed in sport jacket and tie.

"Hi Marty," he said breezily. "June home?"

The talking in the kitchen had stopped. Marty felt them listening. "The name is Mister Hart," Marty said. "And my wife is Missus Hart. And you are on my property—do you have a warrant?"

The cop reddened and his face hardened.

"Then get off my property."

The cop took a deep breath, smiled a tight little smile. "I brought you and the missus some light summer reading," he said, tossing the stapled sheaf of papers into the living room. He turned and walked the brick sidewalk to the street, where he went around an unmarked car, got in, and drove off. Marty closed the door, turned, and saw June in the kitchen doorway. Her face was pale. Marty picked up the papers and glanced over the first page.

"What is it?" June asked.

"They're accusing *you* now. Of dealing. From the look of this, they're doing what Callaghan said they'd do if they want the house. This looks like the start of the seizure process."

Carol went to June, slipped her arm round June's waist and turned her into the kitchen. Carol tried to steer June to the table, but June raised her hand and shook her head.

"This really sucks," Charlie muttered, following Marty and the two women into the kitchen.

Marty looked at Charlie, feeling now a certain camaraderie that had not been there before. It seemed like Charlie and Carol were part of it now. "Yes. And no. Callaghan says that seizure, *then* criminal charges, can complicate things for the prosecutor. In some jurisdictions it has been construed as double jeopardy. He thinks they will pick one and drop the other, because packaging them makes their case more complex—and therefore harder to win. This means they've made a choice. They want the money."

June drew away from Carol's enclosing arm and went to the cabinet. She opened one of the glass doors, removed a glass jar, opened a drawer and removed a tiny brass pipe and a small pair of scissors. She put the pipe and scissors on the table in front of Charlie, opened the jar, put the jar beside the pipe, then went to the gas range and turned on the exhaust fan. The faintly skunky aroma of pot was already filling the kitchen.

Charlie tilted a couple of buds out of the jar into his hand, murmuring, "Beautiful stuff! What a lovely frost." He picked up the scissors and began trimming fragments off the glistening buds onto a piece of paper. He funneled the fragments into the pipe bowl, lit it, and drew the smoke into his lungs. He passed the pipe and the lighter to Carol. They all watched the progress of the pipe around the table. When June inhaled, she passed the pipe on to Marty and rose and went out of the kitchen toward the front hall. Marty watched her leave, then heard her footfalls on the stairs. The pipe was coming back to him again when he heard her descending the stairs. He looked up as she entered the kitchen, naked, holding a stack of folded towels.

"Would you like to join Marty and me in a tub?" she said dreamily. "Marty says they can't touch us in there."

DELUSIONS

Beyond the sloping lawn and the gardens and curving side-walks, across four lanes of street and a ditch and railroad tracks, two women approached the ninth green. Leaving their carts on the apron, they advanced, putters in hand. One positioned herself over a ball and practice-stroked while the other went to the flag. Walton fixed his binoculars on the woman over the ball. She studied the lay of the green between ball and flag, stroked, and watched the ball roll. Walton thought the forty-footer would drop, but it didn't—it rimmed the hole and ran four feet past. The woman looked heavenward.

When Century Software moved into its new headquarters on the west side of the valley Walton's seniority gave him the choice of six vice-presidential offices. He had taken this one not because it was favorably situated to observe golfers, but because its corner windows gave him an unobstructed view along the axis of the valley—the most distinctive features of which were its billiard-table flatness and the miles of stately poplars shading a riverside bike path along the valley's eastern boundary.

He lowered his binoculars and turned to find Kimberly standing before his desk. She carried a sheaf of papers, each with a little red Post-It arrow indicating where he was to affix his signature. "I ordered lunch for six from Tony's," she said, dropping the sheaf on his desk, "to be delivered to the main conference room at noon."

"Six?"

"Tom's in L.A."

"Then why are we having the meeting?"

"I wouldn't know."

He watched Kimberly slide the papers across his desk, turn, and swish out of the office, lazily exaggerating the movement of her plump rump. A message to him: a reminder of what he'd once had and wouldn't have again. Ten assignations and ten orgasms. Or—if you counted hers separately—many more; though, given as she was to tumultuous, multiple orgasms, it was impossible to tell if a single shuddering climax was simply going on and on or if she was finishing one and galloping off into another. Give her twenty-five.

Their adultery had progressed in the span of a few weeks from an annual boss-and-admin lunch to its jarring finish in her apartment. Amateur adulterer as he was, he didn't even consider about how he would end the affair. He'd simply assumed these things, being by their nature transient, more or less ended themselves when the novelty wore off. For that reason, he brought it up with no preamble to gentle the words, while she was after-glowing in his arms. She'd leaped from the bed like he'd just announced a positive outcome to an HIV test; and he'd watched, stunned, as she threw herself into skirt and blouse, all the while screaming, "Get out, get out, get out, get out—" For days thereafter he'd anticipated the inevitable meeting with Hilger, during which he would learn the consequences of sexual harassment in the workplace, and after which he would clean out his desk and slink out the back door to his car, under the shocked gaze of several hundred colleagues, who would line the second and third floor windows to observe his humiliation.

But she did not make Hilger punish him. She punished him herself, by perversely refusing to do the decent thing and resign her position as his administrative assistant. Now she never looked at him except to acknowledge a request, and never smiled when he was present. But, most ominously, her presence beyond the glass wall of his office reminded him constantly that every day he went to work could be his last.

He swiveled his chair around and raised the binoculars to his eyes, found the end of the long line of trees at the lower end of the valley, and panned slowly northward. His gaze swept along the bike path, passing over bicyclists peddling against a background of thick trunks of ancient poplars and patches of blackberry brambles. He lowered the binoculars.

Walton accepted his culpability in the adulterous adventure with Kimberly. Nonetheless, he felt that his adultery was less egregious than his wife's adultery, in part because his had been in hurt and angry reaction to hers, and in part because her adultery had probably been going on for months, and showed no signs of ending any time soon. Not that he actually had the goods on her. His evidence was circumstantial. In fact, when he stepped back from the situation and examined it with the dispassion of a disinterested observer, his suspicions seemed pretty farfetched. The only reliable indication he had was the fact that she seemed to work like hell at avoiding private situations with him; that, and the fact that her avoidance of his affections had begun only after she and her putative lover began working together as a sales-technical team that at times had to travel to make presentations. Travel overnight, in some situations.

The telephone buzzed and Walton swung around. He picked up the handset and Hilger responded to his greeting.

"You got a minute, Walt?"

"Sure," Walton said, as heartily as he could. Meeting with Hilger was always uncomfortable for Walton. He could not

figure out why Hilger regarded him with a distaste that sometimes seemed like outright contempt.

"C'mon down to my office. We need to talk about this
problem I got."

Walton's unease about Kimberly's mental stability made
his heart skip a beat. "What kind of problem?" he asked.

"We'll talk about it when you get here."

Walton heard the click of Hilger ending the conversation.
He picked up his notebook and a pen and walked out of his
office past Kimberly's desk. He turned down the long corridor
to Hilger's office.

Hilger was at his desk, looking out over the golf course
through his binoculars. Walton tapped on the open door.

Hilger waited for half a minute, then lowered his binoculars and pointed to a straight-backed chair in front of his desk.
"Have a seat, Walt. Close the door behind you."

Though Hilger had been with the company for only six
months, Walton had learned how to read his actions. He
knew a good deal about how to interpret Hilger's demeanor.
He knew, for instance, that when Hilger made you wait he
was letting you figure out that he was pissed; as he was when
he sat you down in one of the straight-backed chairs before
his desk, rather than in one of the upholstered chairs that
surrounded the cocktail table. When he did that he was *real*
pissed, and you would have reason to fear you had become
one of his action items. Walton approached the big birch desk
and sat in one of the two chairs and waited.

Another half minute of silence as Hilger panned the binoculars across the golf course. When he spoke, his voice was
uncharacteristically tight and controlled: "I been watching a
couple of women play five through nine. One of 'em is good.
You play golf, Walt?"

"No, I don't."

"I don't play golf either. Though I'm good at it. I learned when I was a kid floggin' Bibles door to door that if you treat something as a game you won't do it well. I don't do anything unless I do it well, and golf is a particularly interesting challenge. It can be a place of business, an exercise for body and mind, an adversarial contest that challenges and builds character, and it can be an arena for the exercise of diplomacy. It's a lot of things, but it isn't a game." He opened a desk drawer and put the binoculars away. "But that's not what I called you about."

Walton watched Hilger open a file folder on his desktop, glanced over a page of scribbled lines, then looked up at Walton.

"Your admin came to me yesterday. She told me you took her to lunch and got her drunk and fucked her. Now, she didn't say rape, which is a good thing for you, but she did say you threatened to fire her if she didn't come across."

Walton had grown pale and he felt light-headed. He drew a breath to respond, but Hilger stopped him with a raised hand. "Walt, before you say anything, let me clear away the smoke so we both see the same things. We both know that if you hadn't been working here when I came on board you wouldn't be here now, 'cause I probably wouldn't have hired you. Not because I think you're a bad person, or that you lack abilities, but because we haven't found a way to communicate with one another. It's probably a simple thing, like we just don't like one another." He shrugged. "That happens. But I don't let feelings get in the way of runnin' this corporation. I wasn't behind this desk for a month before I saw you as the best manager in the place. That's why you're still Vice President of Operations. You're an important cog in the machinery, Walt. Kimberly ain't."

Hilger looked at Walton for several seconds before resuming. "Am I clear on that, Walt? We both see the same picture now, don't we?"

Walton felt light, almost detached from himself. He nodded.

"You sure?"

Walton nodded again.

"But you got to get there from here, so I need to know some things. If you raped her or threatened her, that would be very bad for you, and there's nothing I could do about it. But if you fucked her with her consent? Well, that's not so bad for *you*, but for me it's still pretty bad, because it's 99% of a good reason to can you, *whatever* the circumstances of your liaison with Kimberly. Because you got power over her. Because she works for you." Hilger frowned down at the sheet of paper. "That's the frame of reference for the picture we both see. On the other hand, I have to say I just don't credit her accusation. It doesn't ring true. All accusation, no evidence. For instance, she says on several occasions you forced her to fuck you. I can't believe that. Unless, of course, someone can substantiate it. They can't do that, can they, Walt?"

"No," Walton murmured, "No one—" But he went silent when Hilger raised his hand again.

"As I said, it doesn't ring true to me. I don't believe you're the kind of man that takes advantage of an admin like that. So what does the world know about this—situation? That you took her out to lunch." Hilger shrugged. "No harm in that—a good boss does that once in a while, and I view you as a good boss. Anybody see you with her at lunch? Or anyplace else? Has anybody that knows you seen you with her?"

Walton slowly shook his head. "I—don't think so," he said weakly.

"Yeah," Hilger said, "the more I think about it the more inclined I am to think she told the truth about the lunch, but she's makin' up the fucking. Or maybe she's delusional. Could be that, couldn't it?"

Walton opened his mouth to speak.

But Hilger held up his hand once again and shook his head. "Don't need to say anything right now. In fact, if I was you I'd wait a day or two to respond—to make sure my response was clear and unambiguous. And that I fully understood consequences. Because if it turns out she *ain't* delusional it's gonna mean you fucked her and—well, I think you seen the picture I see, and understand that I'm gonna do what I gotta do. Neither one of us wants that." He fell silent and studied Walton, who looked away. "This is stressful, Walt. So I want you to go home and think about this. Take tomorrow off as well. When you return you can tell me if you think Kimberly's being delusional. I'll know what to do then. I don't want to influence you, but I can't help hoping that's what you're gonna say—that she's delusional." Hilger turned his chair enough to see the golf course, wet now, under a darkening sky. "We got a big fall coming up, Walt, and I need the skills of a first-rate operations guy a hell of a lot more'n I need the skills of an admin." He turned back to his desk, picked up the file folder, and closed it. "Now that you're here we might as well talk about somethin' else I been plannin' to talk to you about for two weeks, but haven't gotten around to yet. The sexual harassment meetings. They're comin' up again next quarter and HR tells me you're the only V.P. who hasn't conducted the meetings. I'd like for you to go over to HR this afternoon and tell 'em you're gonna do it this year." His smile was thin and humorless. "I think you might have the right experience for this, Walt."

THE GATES OF SODOM

A sigh of wind through cedars followed him down the path to the road, where he turned toward the town. At the edge of town he stopped at Miller's Grocery and bought a quart of milk. When he came to the squat concrete-block structure next to the Shell station he unlocked the door and entered. At his desk he raised the carton to his lips. The cold coursed down through his chest and spread out inside him. He pulled a drawer open and removed a ledger. Inside was a sheaf of bills, which he spread across the desk. He gazed gloomily at the scraps of paper, then began picking local bills out of the pile. Putting them aside, he studied the rest.

If the paper supplier, the power company, or the telephone company cut him off he was out of business, so he added their bills to the must-pay pile. He paper-clipped the handful that remained, and, putting them aside, opened the checkbook and began writing. When the account was zeroed he examined the pieces of paper remaining in the must-pay pile. He put them under a paperweight in the center of his desk, to remind him that he had to find some money in the next few days, somehow. The rest of the unpaid bills he put between pages of the journal.

He looked at his watch. Only ten-thirty. He got up and went into the composing room and looked at the ads on Shirley's worktable. His notes on the Tedder Hardware ad were paper-clipped to Shirley's layout, reminding him that he had to finish his piece on the Tedder family before Monday afternoon. Tedder's great-great-grandfather had been the first settler on the island, and for years had rowed his homemade skiff across four miles of open water to the mainland every week with butter and cheese to sell at the settlement; he had advertised for a wife, paid her fare to Seattle, and, after marrying her, had carried her across that open water in his skiff. The article was shaping up. It would get a couple of nice ads out of Tedder.

He reviewed Shirley's layout—not that she'd let him change anything. But he was not thinking about how to improve the ad. He was killing time until noon, when he'd let himself get a cigarette from the pack in the upper-right drawer of his desk. He'd last smoked a cigarette the night before, at midnight, as he'd stumbled home in the rain.

To divert his mind from the cigarette he would deny himself until noon, he got his coat, went outside, and walked past the Shell station and the theater and Mike's Café and the tourist shops that had once been vacation houses. Immediately to the rear of this line of old structures was the bluff that overlooked a muddy tide flat and the long reach of the Sound. When he came to Mary's Tavern, which was at the highest point in the town, he stopped and looked north—over four streets of service stations and cafés and real estate offices and boutiques and galleries and a half-dozen cross streets of the same stuff.

The northwesterly had brought the black sky closer, and the wind was picking up, bringing with it the mare's tail of a squall. He thought about taking Clyde's skiff out to fish the tidal rip on the south side of the island, but knew he wouldn't. For the last two years he had been making excuses to himself about being too busy to get out on he water. Looking through the front window of the tavern, he saw Mary leaning over the sink behind the bar, her eyes on the television glowing on the wall opposite the bar. He pushed the door open and went inside.

Mary drew her hands from the soapy water and picked up a towel. "Hello, Charlie. Coffee?"

"Yeah," he murmured, settling himself on a barstool. He watched her move ponderously to the end of the bar and pour a cup and return. She looked damp and overheated, and gray strings of hair hung out of the bun knotted at the back of her head. She had been obese for so many years that few remembered her as the slim long-haired hippie who had married first him, and then middle-aged Calvin. But Charlie remembered: she had been his wife for five years when she decided Calvin was a better opportunity, and she'd cuckolded Charlie for six months before he figured things out. She was right about Calvin—he was a better opportunity.

"You seen my hat, Mary?"

She pointed to the wall behind him.

He looked into the mirror and saw the hat hanging on one of the hooks beneath the television. He slid off the stool and got the hat and put it on and returned to the bar.

"Gimme a cigarette, Mary."

She took a pack of Marlboros from the countertop behind her and slid it across the bar and went back to washing glasses. "I read Radford's letter," she said.

He lit the cigarette.

"He's a weird dude." She wiped her hands on a towel and picked her cigarette out of the ash tray and lifted her cup of coffee.

Charlie shoved his untouched cup aside. "Think I'd rather have a beer, Mary."

She drew a beer and placed it on the bar. He slid a five-dollar bill toward her. She made change and went back to washing the glasses, glancing from time to time at the television glowing and murmuring behind Charlie, who smoked his cigarette and looked at himself in the mirror.

જ

"You been here twenty-five years—I'd've thought you knew him," Tedder said.

Charlie shook his head. "Never met him."

"You'll learn more about him if you talk to folks up in Coupville. He's better known there than here."

"Yeah, I'll do that. But you're his neighbor."

The doorbell tinkled and Tedder rose and went around his desk, leaving Charlie sitting in the armchair. Charlie had come with a proof of Tedder's ad, and had begun probing Tedder about Radford. He watched Tedder approach the counter and talk to a young man, then disappear behind a gondola display of carpenter's tools. A moment later he reappeared carrying a bag of nails. He took money, made change, and chatted for a moment with the young man, then returned to the office and settled into his swivel chair.

"He comes across in his letters as a bit of a zealot," Charlie said, to bring them back to Radford.

"Zealot? I believe the right word is nut. But he'll respect your limits if you tell him what they are. We've been neighbors for fifty years and I've never had a conversation with him about religion or politics. Because he learned I'll always turn it off."

"You mentioned his estrangement from his sons," Charlie said. "Was it religion?"

"What's this about, Charlie?"

"Background."

"For what? Hope you're not planning to quote me in some article about Radford. What I said is private."

"It's just background. I'm trying to understand where he's coming from."

Another of Radford's letters was waiting for Charlie when he returned to his office.

Dear Editor,
    I see that you put my letter in your paper last week, I suppose to ridicule me, but I will not be turned away by ridicule, because we are at the Gates of Sodom where the Lords Angels came to warn Lot to take his family away so they could escape from the fire which the Lord poured upon the city of Sodom. That fire is what awaits you and the other abominations like homosexuals and fornicators and developers that has invaded our peaceful island.
    God is giving signs that he is angry at what is happening but it is not to late to open your hearts to Him. The homosexuals is bringing sodomy and AIDS among us and the artists bringing drugs and the atheists blasphemy and the hippies sloth and the worst of them is the developers poisoning the land and loving only money. This island is filling with evil people that hate God's peace and are an abomination in the eyes of the Lord. We have to drive the abominations out or we will die like them, for God is saying in all the signs that He will kill them and He will consume the town in fire and leave only ashes.
    Believe on Christ and come together with me and march with me in the town and tell the developers and fornicators and sodomites and abortionists that we are taking our island back and we will drive them out.
                                Yours in Christ
                                Andrew Radford

"Hey, Shirley, " Charlie shouted. He swung around in his chair.

Shirley was standing in the doorway wiping her hands on a shop rag. Her plump body was buttoned into a set of overalls. She looked annoyed, as usual.

Charlie waved the letter, grinning. "Stop the presses, I want this in."

"The presses stopped on their own and they're not going to start unless you get that slider, which broke like I told you it was going to."

"You didn't order one?"

"You know I didn't order one—Archer's has had us on COD for months."

"Call Archer and tell him I want to pick one up right away. I'll take a check. But forget that for a minute and look at this. There's a new angle."

She read the letter, then looked up at him. "You aren't gonna publish this, are you?"

"People are interested, you've heard the talk."

"Charlie, you're not H.L. Mencken and this ain't *The Baltimore Sun*. People open *The Independence* to find out about weddings and specials at the Safeway, not to read threats from religious crackpots." She brushed a wisp of gray hair out of her eyes. "There's no context for this. When you publish it without context it's just holding the weirdness of a poor old crazy up for ridicule."

"You're wrong. His ideas are what a lot of people around here have been talking about for a long time. He just says it more directly."

"His *ideas* were worn out five hundred years ago."

"C'mon up, Shirley, Radford's jihad isn't against people."

"You're the editor of this little shopper, so I guess you can play journalist all you want, but I put the goddamned thing out and I can't without that goddamned slider. Get me another one or you got no newspaper, mister journalist."

"Okay, okay."

❧

The island's art community came to the island in the Age of Aquarius to create a new order. And married, and divorced, and married again, and as often as not made the same mistakes again, swapping wives and husbands and squabbling among themselves, and saw the stresses of family life and of earning a living erode their solidarity. Over the years they melded one by one into the larger community. Now they worked at the lumber yard, and operated the gift boutique on Main Street, the art gallery next door, a gas station on the road to the ferry terminal, Mary's Tavern, the local newspaper, taught in the high school, worked at the Safeway, and they were calloused carpenters and leathery fishermen. But some of them still came together regularly, still affected the outward aspects of the solidarity that had once united them—long pony-tailed hair, droopy bandito moustaches, tie-dye blouses, beads—and some still spoke the dialect of that earlier time, still adhered to the tattered ethos that had brought them together. The rites of that ethos were their cultural foundation—the annual theater production, the annual art show, and the last-Friday-of-the-month literary readings in the back of Mary's Tavern, which were readings initiated twenty years before by Calvin and Charlie as a joke. On reading nights the aging Aquarians gathered in the back room around tables covered with beer bottles and listened to the poet in one of themselves or a minor novelist on a book-promotion tour. Charlie was always there, presiding.

On this Friday night the poet was a young Bukowski imitator who was also a newcomer to the island. To prepare himself for his reading, and to establish his reputation, he'd smoked a J and downed a pint of vodka and puked in the middle of his first poem. Like Bukowski. Unlike Bukowski, however, he was unable to continue. He passed out and Larry and Dennis and young Tedder dragged him over to the wall and laid him out while Charlie placated Mary, who threatened once again to terminate the island's cultural life by terminating the public literary readings in Mary's Tavern. As Paul, the evening man, cleaned up the mess and Mary grumbled and put a Joan Baez tape in the player behind the bar, most of the twenty of so patrons of art wandered to the pool tables and the bar in the front of the tavern. Charlie remained, with Shirley and Timmy and Larry and Dennis.

"Well," Timmy Tedder murmured defensively, "like, I just worked for him was all. He paid me good, even give me his '61 Chevy pickup at the end of the summer—a bonus. But he never said nuthin' to me about no religious stuff or gays or stuff like that."

Dennis swelled indignantly: as usual Timmy missed the point. He gave up on Timmy and focused his anger on Charlie. "What I can't understand, Charlie, is how can you print that vomit?"

Charlie belched. "You're taking it personal, Dennis. When he talks about gays—"

Shirley pushed back from the table and rose. She jerked her coat off the back of the chair.

Charlie looked up at her. "Where you going?"

"I'm sick of listening to talk about Radford. I'm going home and watch TV."

"I'll walk you," Charlie said. "Maybe we can do a tub." He put his hand on her hip.

She shoved it off. "No thanks. Tonight it's TV and then sleep."

Charlie grinned and watched her march through the swirl of cigarette smoke to the door.

ຎ

By the time Charlie published the third Radford letter the entire community was aware of Radford's message. Even the newest and fastest growing element of the community—the commuters who lived a suburban life in clusters of new houses situated between the town and the ferry dock and who knew little about local issues—entered discussions about Radford's Old Testament zeal. The town's two ministers, one a Methodist, the other a Baptist, protested mildly to Charlie, saying they worried that exploitation of religious bigotry would create hatred and division in the community. Charlie was surprised. Exploitation? He spoke earnestly of the responsibility of the press to both inform and to be a voice for the citizens of the community. The preachers departed, unconvinced of the importance of citizen Andrew Radford's ideas.

When nothing came from Radford in the days following publication of his third letter, Charlie became uneasy. A momentum of expectation had developed. For the first time in the newspaper's history, people waited for *The Independence* to come out. In advertising and in the number of papers put on the street this edition would be the biggest Charlie had published. To maintain momentum it was imperative that he print something from Radford. He was greatly relieved when another Radford letter came on Wednesday morning. He stopped everything and told Shirley to recompose the *Letters-to-the-Editor* section, and to set it up opposite Tedder's full page of advertising. Shirley muttered and slammed things around and did as she was told. They worked late, but they got the paper out.

Charlie was tired but happy when he locked the office and headed for Mary's, with a half-dozen copies of *The Independence* tucked under his arm. By then, hundreds of islanders were reading the newest Radford missive.

Dear Editor,
    I will write this letter anyway, knowing you probably won't have the courage to print it for your heart is hardened against my message of hope and love. I know you fornicators and developers and homosexuals ridicules me and my mission, but I have received many thankful letters from those God fearing citizens which has been silent while they watched their fair town become another Sodom. Well they are not silent now. When I talk to them as I do every day I weep with joy that the Lord has made me bring His message of hope for there is still hope to avoid the fate of Sodom. We can save ourselves by marching in the town and driving the sodomites out.
    Christians! Join me and your Christian neighbors at the post office parking lot on the 15th of November at noon and we will march together under Gods banner of Love and drive the Fornicators and Sodomites and developers out of our town.
                    Yours in Christ
                    Andrew Radford

By the next morning everyone was talking about Radford's letter. A few had lost their sense of humor about Radford's message, but everyone wondered who among them was sending all those letters of support that Radford claimed.

Charlie's weekly sold out. Those who'd never before even looked at *The Independence* sought it out. And Charlie did not have to call advertisers on Thursday and Friday to beg them to place ads for the next week. They called him.

On Friday evening Charlie held forth as usual as the master of ceremonies at the literary reading—soberly, for the first time in years. That evening he walked Shirley home and they soaked in the old redwood tub, and he slept with her for the first time in many weeks. He left her bed before first light and walked home, got his old pickup started, and drove down to the marina. There he bought a dozen live herring and while it was still dark got Clyde's skiff ready and was motoring out as a low gray sky became drizzle and then rain. The clunky skiff lurched into a choppy sea when it rounded the point and rain slanted into his face, stinging his cheeks. He motored the two miles along the coast to the tidal rip that snaked off the southern tip of the island down toward the middle of the Sound, and when he was in the flotsam of the rip—in dirty swirls of foam, brown tendrils of kelp, bits of drift-wood, wads of uprooted eel grass, chunks of Styrofoam—all tossing and heaving on the choppy sea—he idled the engine down and rigged his rod with a four-ounce weight five feet above a flasher and a single herring and began trolling along the rip. He caught a pair of six-pounders in a half hour and was motoring in with the wind at his back when the first of the Sunday fishermen from Everett and Seattle appeared in their cruisers.

In the mail on Monday Charlie found another Radford letter, as well as a pile of letters from all over the island expressing disgust, humor, outrage, bewilderment. On Wednesday Charlie published Radford's letter and a letter from the Methodist preacher abhorring the bigotry in Radford's message. On the same page Charlie published an editorial defending the publication of Radford's letters, which he termed "articles from a writer with another point of view, one that may be different, one that many find repugnant, but one that has as much right as any to be heard."

The response to that edition of *The Independence*, the last before Radford's march, was even greater than the week before. On Wednesday evening Mary's was packed, the crowd excited and exuberant, the talk centered on the sudden and amazing emergence of Radford's movement. On Thursday the tavern was even busier. Mary held the kitchen open until nearly midnight and she herself worked a double shift. The festivity on Friday night was spiced by a counterpoint of tension. By midnight only the drunks remained, gathered in a group at a table beneath the television, speculating boisterously about whom they would see marching with Radford the next day. Charlie, sober and pink-cheeked and pleased with life, observed the shouting from a barstool beside Shirley. At midnight he walked her home and they soaked in the redwood tub.

ひ

By ten o'clock Saturday morning the shops were open and pedestrians appeared on Main Street. Mary's filled up. Charlie finished his coffee and slid off his bar stool and returned to the newspaper office for the camera bag.

Pedestrian traffic along the street was heavier than Charlie had ever seen, even in the bright days of August. Walking up the street between crowded sidewalks, looking for backgrounds, he shot a roll, reloaded the Nikon, and entered the crowd, where he took out his notebook and began interviewing. A few minutes later he heard a silence working its way down the street. A block away a lone figure came into view from a side street. The figure, a man, turned and walked toward him, holding a sign above his head.

Charlie stepped off the curb and looked through the viewfinder. The long lens, flattening the scene, showed a small man with sloping shoulders and white hair, foreshortened against a line of people. A self-conscious hint of a smile gave his leathery face a grandfatherly appearance. Charlie turned the zoom ring and brought the face close and isolated against an out-of-focus background. He clicked off several frames, then lowered the camera and stepped out of the old man's way.

The watchers lining the sidewalks had been quiet, but now a murmur rose, and shouts and laughter came out of the crowd: "Give 'em hell, Radford!" and "Hey Radford, I smell brimstone—look out behind you!" Each shout was followed by a ripple of laughter. Radford sailed on through them, holding his sign aloft, holding that embarrassed smile on his lips. As he turned the corner at the end of the street he looked back at the crowd that had already dismissed him; its cohesion gone, it was dissolving now to individuals, each with a different mission. Gathering children, they drifted off toward cars and shops, or clustered to converse for a neighborly moment before getting on with the chores of another Saturday. Radford moved into a side street and brought the sign down off his shoulder. He trudged up the gently sloping hill past small cottages with big yards that petered out against grassy ditches and graveled driveways.

Charlie snapped a few more frames, then turned and walked back toward the street of shops and restaurants. With the exception of a few individuals moving purposefully toward stores or cars, the crowd had vanished. He stuffed his notebook into his jacket pocket, put the Nikon back into its nest in the camera bag, and made his way to Mary's. Entering, he paused in the smoky open space between pool tables and bar, and decided he did not want to listen to a rehash of the morning, which was what he would get if he went to the back room, packed as it was with the lunch crowd. So he climbed up on a bar stool and signaled to Mary to bring him a beer.

He lit a cigarette and savored his discovery that after all these years a fragment of journalistic pride still dwelled within him. As he smoked and looked at himself in the mirror he reflected on that moment when the old man emerged alone from the side street with his sign. No friend, no neighbor, none of the brothers and sisters of his church had been there to join him, or even to greet him. Not even that rejection had dissuaded the old man; he did what he said he was going to do. Charlie admired the old man's certainty.

Communing thus with the image in the mirror, he listened to a piece from The Doors, *circa* 1967, and wished that someone from the community had had the balls, or the bad taste, to stand there with the old man at the gates of Sodom.

WEDDING PARTY

Two orgasms—increasing the number of his illicit climaxes (in eleven sexual encounters with a half-dozen women who were not his wife) during his twenty-three years of marriage, to twelve. The two with Shree were recent—the rest, with his second cousin Alicia in 1980, the neighbor in their first apartment building, their first au pair, and the other two whom he knew so briefly that he could not really remember how they looked—all were so long ago they should not be counted. But in the interest of precision, he did count them—giving him an average of zero-point-four-five illicit orgasms per year. A miniscule disloyalty, Morgan mused (doing the arithmetic in his head as he followed the lawn mower back across the yard), when compared to his many loyal orgasms—some four thousand, he calculated.

Specifically, his illicit orgasms were less than three-tenths of one percent of the total of all his orgasms, which meant that he was ninety-nine and seven-tenths percent loyal. On the other hand (his commitment to honesty forcing this stern self reproach), a high loyalty ratio does not mitigate disloyalty, not even trivial disloyalty, which, it seemed to him, is what we're talking about here. That said, neither should his low disloyalty ratio brand him with the big red A. In fact, the percentages showed him to be simply a man of human fallibility, but one who'd learned from his mistakes. Yes, he generously owned, he could make a mistake now and then, as even the saints made mistakes once in a while.

Perspective: that was the thing. To understand the seriousness of a problem, you have to put it in perspective, which means you have to quantify the problem and place it in a frame of reference. How else can you understand it? For example, if you chain-smoked cigarettes on, say, twelve of the last eighty-four-hundred days, it's not likely that your health would be noticeably impaired by that activity. On the other hand, if you chain-smoked cigarettes throughout all of the last eighty-four-hundred days it's very likely the cigarettes would have destroyed your health. Perspective. Moderation.

His disloyalty, he told himself, was the consequence of unfortunate convergence of opportunity, unsatisfied appetite, and—he admitted it—a momentary ethical weakness. But of course a large part of the motivation for his momentary ethical weakness was that element of unsatisfied appetite. How long had Jane been sexually indifferent to him? For years—though he had to admit that until this last year or so she'd always performed her wifely duty with an acceptable level of attention, if not enthusiasm—attention that wasn't even on her radar these days.

Morgan switched the lawn mower off and pushed it to the brick sidewalk and around the garage to the tool shed, then returned to the backyard to tackle another of the several gardening chores Jane had assigned to him as his part of the wedding preparations. The next activity on the list was planting twenty flats of bright summer annuals in the gardens along the back fence, which was to be the backdrop for the wedding ceremony.

That afternoon with Shree had been just like this one. During most of the week since that afternoon, she was seldom out of his mind. Even now, as he wished it had never happened, he longed to be with her, to make it happen again.

He climbed the two stairs to the deck, kicked his shoes off, entered the kitchen, and filled the tea kettle.

❧

"Reverend Standish, this is my husband, Morgan."

Morgan rose and offered his hand to the young man.

"Jim," Reverend Standish said, bobbing his head. "Please call me Jim."

"And this is our groom, James."

James pushed himself to his feet and, looking sardonically at his mother, offered a limp hand to Reverend Standish. "Groom? For God's sake, Mom, we've been cohabiting for two years."

Smiling uncertainly, Reverend Standish glanced at Jane. But Jane had turned to Lynn, who waited, puffy and pregnant, on the sofa.

"And this is the bride, Lynn Irvin. Lynn and James met at Oregon State, where they're both students."

"Former students," James said, to no one.

"*I'm* still a student," Lynn corrected him. "*I* intend to finish."

James shrugged and fell into a slouch on the sofa beside her. He jammed his hands into his jeans and looked up at Reverend Standish.

"We're all a little tense," Jane soothed. "Won't you sit down, Jim?" She pointed helpfully at the armchair that she'd situated across the cocktail table from James and Lynn, which positioned Reverend Standish, as counselor, suitably superior to the bride and groom.

Reverend Standish sat, crossed his legs, assumed his professional demeanor, and proceeded to the business at hand. "This promise you're about to make to one another—though it signals a very important event in your lives—is also a promise to God, which is every bit as important, because—"

"We're atheists," James said, crossing his arms.

Reverend Standish glanced around, as if seeking some indicator of which way the wind was blowing in this house.

James ignored his mother's look of irritation: "And as you can see—" nodding sidewise at Lynn "—she's knocked up. So the promise has already been delivered. So to speak."

Lynn looked sidelong at him, with a hint of a smile shaping her prominent lips.

"Would you like a cup of tea?" Jane asked. "Or perhaps a glass of wine."

"I think—wine please."

"I'll help," Morgan said, and followed her. "Where'd you find him?" he whispered, when they'd passed through the swinging door into the kitchen. "I was hoping for someone with a little more gravitas—a little taller perhaps, gray at the temples, granite chin, backward collar. That sort of thing. This child is still popping his zits and training his hair."

"Don't start," she hissed.

He watched her open a bottle of wine and take down two glasses. "Pour me one, too."

She got another glass.

"What church?"

"The New Christian Evangelical Church."

"Evangelical? This might be more fun than I thought. Does he know she's a Jew?"

"She's an atheist."

"To some of the folks on his side of the religious divide, a Jew can no more become a non-Jew than a black man can become white."

Her lips were a thin line. "He knows, and he does not care."

"A fundamentalist, maybe-anti-Semitic, evangelical preacher—did you ask if his congregation is associated with the Aryan Nations? Wow. Sanctioning the holy matrimony of a relapsed Episcopalian and an apostate Jew, while her yarmulked father, Hymie Irvin, Torah in hand, swings his incense burner and—"

"Hymie doesn't even own a yarmulke."

"These Jews are tricky. They can fool you. One minute they're scarfing ham and bacon and fucking nice Christian girls, just like decent people, and the next they're off in some synagogue mumbling their evil incantations and drinking the blood of Christian babies."

"Besides, Jim told me—"

"Jim?"

"Yes, Jim. You heard him. He's too young to be called Reverend, and he knows it."

"Jim seems a bit undignified. How about *Brother* Jim?"

"What's gotten into you?" she asked. She raised her glass, drank half its content, and poured it full again. "Jim considers this an ecumenical situation. He's already told me he'll secularize parts of the ceremony. And he's not anti-Semitic; he's a gentle, sensitive, serious-minded young man."

Morgan grinned. He was enjoying this evening more than he'd thought he would. "Where'd you find him? Don't tell me: the Yellow Pages, under 'Weddings: Ecumenical.'"

She glared at him, her lips so tightly compressed they disappeared.

He laughed. "It *was* the Yellow Pages!"

"Listen, I've been all over the north end and he was the first one I found who said he'd perform the ceremony we want. He's the only game in town, so take him a glass of wine and be nice while I get my notebook."

With a wine glass in each hand Morgan pushed through the kitchen door. Reverend Standish stopped speaking and looked up with a wide smile.

"It seems that we have something in common," Reverend Standish said.

"We're all atheists," James drawled.

Reverend Standish reddened. "That's not what I meant. I was talking about the poetry—we have poetry in common. I asked James if he'd let me read some of his poems."

"Don't forget tolerance," Lynn said.

"Of course—tolerance," Reverend Standish added. "We agreed that one has to try to understand the spiritual content of the other fellow's belief—or woman's, of course—" nodding at Lynn "—and not get tangled up in the connotation of the message. That's really what I was trying to say."

"That means he doesn't believe in fairy tales and forest nymphs, either."

"That's putting it a bit too strongly, I think," Reverend Standish demurred. "While I do try to maintain a healthy level of skepticism—as a matter of principle; an open mind, so to speak—I was trying to make the point that when you look closely at belief systems you find amazing similarity. Some belief systems have coexisted for thousands of years, side by side, and it's inevitable that there's been a lot of borrowing. It's only in the connotation of the beliefs that the more fearful among us find a rationale for extremism and distrust."

"He means that when people start believing the myths are literally true, trivial differences become important. Take the virgin birth, for instance." At this James laid his hand on Lynn's belly. "A very common event in history, it turns out. If you believe all the legends and myths."

Lynn giggled.

"That's sort of what I was getting at—" Reverend Standish said, taking the glass of wine that Morgan offered. "I'm so glad Jane called me. Your son and daughter-in-law-to-be are most stimulating. And believe me, it's very refreshing to be able to talk openly to open-minded people." A rueful smile. "Of course a person in my position shouldn't be talking this way at all— it feels awfully wicked—but I must say it excites me, and it makes me recall those evenings of fierce disputation about poetry and beauty and virtue and truth, which used to occupy my classmates and me in the tavern down the hill from the seminary. I've missed the camaraderie and openness that attended those explorations. That freedom to—well, to speak freely, if you know what I mean. I guess I'd forgotten how much I enjoyed the freedom to say things that I just can't say around my flock. They're rather conservative on social matters, you know. And very, very conservative on matters of faith. They would not be sympathetic with this conversation."

"You seem rather—well, liberal in your views."

Reverend Standish smiled wanly. "I needed a job, and this one was open. I confess that sometimes it is a bit trying."

Jane had entered the room with a glass of wine and her notebook and seated herself on the sofa beside Lynn. "That is certainly very interesting," she said, opening the notebook. "And it reminds me that we need to discuss the details of the ceremony. As I told you yesterday, Lynn and James want a ceremony that is as open as possible."

"Oh, certainly," Reverend Standish said. "Open."

"I don't want any mention of God," James said.

Jane darted a look of annoyance at James, who once more ignored her.

Reverend Standish frowned thoughtfully. "Well—it's sort of a religious ceremony. Most people expect you to refer to

God at least a few times in sermons and wedding ceremonies—otherwise what's the authority behind the demands
you're making? How about if I mention God a couple of times
but not Jesus? You know, God in a generic sense? That seems
more ecumenical than scriptural."

"I agree," Jane said. "We definitely need to mention God.
People will expect it."

James crossed his arms and said: "Well, *I* don't agree."

"I don't agree, either," Morgan said genially. He didn't
care, actually, but he wanted to encourage the discussion, for
it was amusing.

Jane glared at Morgan. "The guests will expect some reference to God."

"It's James' and Lynn's wedding," Morgan reminded Jane.
"They should be the ones to decide if God is invited."

"James does not care about this, he's just being difficult."

"Oh, sure," James said. "Whenever *James* disagrees, he's
being difficult. *James* couldn't possibly have an opinion based
on anything more principled than being difficult."

"Let's move on," Jane said through thin lips. "How much
time should we allocate for the ceremony?"

"It's their wedding, not ours," Morgan said, unwilling to
move on.

Jane ignored Morgan. "How long do you expect it to take?"

Reverend Standish cleared his throat. "Umm. Ten minutes?"

"Ten minutes!" James said. "If you cut out all that crap
about God it shouldn't take more than thirty seconds."

"Why don't we compromise?" Morgan suggested. "How
about ninety seconds? A minute and a half, once the bride and
groom are in position, ready to receive Reverend Standish's
benediction."

"Jim," Jim reminded Morgan. "And—uh, it's really not a
benediction."

"Right. Facing Jim."

"Ten minutes will be perfect," Jane said icily. "Now, about the physical arrangement. When the band starts the wedding march, Hymie will escort the bride out the kitchen door, past the hot tub, and down the stairs."

"I see a serious problem," Morgan said. "Hymie's a Jew. Can he escort the bride in a Christian ceremony, even if she's Jewish?"

℘

Shree, carrying an empty wine stem, left the circle formed by Jack, James, Reverend Standish, and Bill, and went across the grass to the stairs leading up to the deck. She passed the covered hot tub, where Morgan stood with Lynn, Hymie, Jane, and Jeannie, listening to Norma detail the sexual abuse her new boss had already begun heaping on her. Shree's glance met Morgan's as she passed him and entered the kitchen.

In his peripheral vision (he dared not actually look at her) Morgan observed through the window that Shree had filled her stem and turned and was leaning against the island in the middle of the kitchen. She seemed to be looking his way as she raised the stem to her lips.

"Why do you think it was a sexual advance?" Jane asked her sister, Norma. "It could have been just what it sounded like—a thank you."

"Oh, you can tell," Norma said knowingly. "They always make it sound so innocent. 'You did a great job on that presentation. I'm gonna reward you with a nice lunch.' Yeah, right—their hot sausage between your buns in a motel room."

Morgan drank down his wine. "Anybody care for another?"

Hymie handed Morgan his empty glass. "Some of that Yakima Merlot." He turned his attention back to Norma.

"You asked, so I'm gonna tell you. It's too thin—a lunch invitation's not a cause for action. Not by itself. Of course, if there's been an underlying, and provable, pattern of sexually abusive behavior, of which this incident is exemplary—well, then you might have something to see a lawyer about."

"Anyone else?" Morgan asked. The women ignored him, so he turned away and entered the back door.

Shree looked at him. "Hi."

"Hi yourself," he said. He placed the two wine glasses on the counter and picked up the bottle of Merlot.

She faced him, holding her glass at her lips. "I like Lynn. She's nice, and so smart. I wish I'd gone to college like her and James."

"Yes, she is," he said. Yeah, smart; like a box of rocks.

"And cute."

"You bet." Cute? She's *pregnant*, not cute; though Morgan had to admit that before her pregnancy he had indeed thought of Lynn as cute—and very sexy. Then the prominent fullness of her lips was alluring, not coarsening, and her body was athletic, resilient, and suggestive of sexual energy, not sedentarily puffy, damp, and breathless.

His attention was drawn to Shree's lips lingering at the lip of her wine glass. Her lips were thin, not full. He was deeply stirred by remembrance of standing thigh-deep in the steaming hot tub, of looking down mesmerized at the sight of his cock gliding into another kind of heat. "Yeah, she's cute," he agreed, suddenly needing to say *something*, even if his voice had gone trembly. Shree's thin lips, still coquettishly toying with the lip of the wine glass, stretched into the faintest hint of a smile. A knowing smile? Was she reading his mind? The thought thrilled and alarmed him.

"I suppose—I ought to get back to the party," he mumbled.

Her smile—was she telling him something? Or was it merely the neutral word play of a sister-in-law? But it did not matter what kind of smile it was, he'd already decided one time was all he could bear; for there was no way this was going any farther. He'd known that eight days before, as she drove off in the rain. So why in heaven's name had he followed her into the kitchen, where he knew they would be alone, if not to encourage *some*thing? Was he really just fetching Hymie a drink, like a good host would do for any guest? And saying "Hi" to her—was that simply a greeting to another guest? Yes, that was all he was doing—being a good host.

"I thought that's where we already were," she smiled. "You know—at the party."

He grinned foolishly.

"Standing around out there makes me cold. That's why I came inside. To get warm."

"It's sweater weather," he agreed in a trembly voice.

"I don't know how Hymie can stand it in that Hawaiian shirt and those shorts and flip-flops. He doesn't seem to even notice the cold."

"Yeah, I noticed that—that he doesn't notice the cold."

"That was the first thing I noticed about him," she amplified.

Morgan noticed that her conversation was as empty as a ping-pong ball. A random walk of words. Butterflies of sounds—set loose to attract his attention and keep him there beside her? Or was she just responding like any bored guest to the inane words of an inane host? But he's always thought that inanity was her intellectual apex.

"He's really a nice guy. He talks to you like being a lawyer's no big deal. He's not stuck up or nothing." Her agreeable smile widened. "And his ponytail's so cute. I love it, even if it's gray and he ain't got no hair on top. Jack said he looks like an old man tryin' to be a kid. But I don't think so. I like him."

She liked everyone, apparently. Except her husband, Jack.

"And he's smart. You gotta be smart to be a lawyer."

"He's one smart guy all right," Morgan agreed.

"God, I want to do a tub right now."

Morgan's mouth went dry, and he was suddenly conscious of how difficult it was to move his tongue. "Me too," he said thickly.

"Just *us*."

He went light-headed, put his hand on the counter to steady himself, and heard himself follow her lead, as if she was the Pied Piper and he was a rat: "Me too."

"You didn't call me."

"I—wanted to," he said, aware that he spoke both the truth and a lie, "but I didn't think you wanted me to."

Incredulously: "You didn't think I *wanted* you to?"

Weakly: "No."

"Did you think I give blow jobs to just anybody I run into in a hot tub? Like I do that as a *favor*, for God's sake? Like, 'I've got an extra blow job here, do you want it?'"

Oh Christ.

"I thought you liked me. 'Cause that's the way you *look* at me. Even right now. Especially like right now."

"I do? I mean, of course I do. Like you, I mean. Honestly."

Her voice softer, and tentative: "Really?"

"Oh yes." Oh Christ, what was he saying? And why, why, *why* the fucking hell was he saying it?

"I wish we were in the hot tub right now. Alone. With you in me." She smiled coyly. "Either end—you could choose."

Oh Christ.

"Will you call me?"

He felt his head going up and down when he desperately wanted it to go side to side.

"Promise me."

Still nodding, he said, "Okay."

"When? Tomorrow?"

He drew a deep breath. "Will—Jack—be home?"

"You want *me* to call *you*?"

"Yes." Oh Christ, oh Christ, oh Christ. *That* was the Rubicon, and he didn't even see the water. He couldn't stand it any longer. "Shree, I've got to get back to the party."

"I want a kiss first."

Incredulously: "Here?"

She smiled. "You're so funny. No. In the hall."

He looked out the window, saw pony-tailed, Hawaiian-shirted Hymie enjoying the encirclement of women, and beyond the circle, fat Jack and his son and Reverend Jim and the others on the grass. Shree, leaning against the counter, watched him with big eyes. She stepped away from the counter and sauntered toward the hall. He followed on legs that felt as wooden as stilts. And as soon as he rounded the corner into the darkness of the foyer she engulfed him.

Morgan stumbled out onto the deck with an erection that had to be sticking out in front of him a foot, and a mildly quivering wine glass in each hand; and saw that Hymie had left the circle of women, who were happily occupied now by a discussion of Lynn's wedding gown. Morgan went down the stairs and joined the men, who stood in a circle on the lawn where the deck lighting faded into darkness. He handed one of the wine glasses to Hymie.

"So, to top it off," Bill was saying, "this pimply-faced twit simpers 'I guess I forgot to order the books. But I'll order five if you can come back next week.' Can you imagine? A fucking five-hour drive to appear in a fourth-rate chain store in a nowhere mall in an end-of-the-road fishing village on the Oregon coast and asks me to do it *again*? By showing *up* in that horse pasture to sign a couple of books I increased the mall population by ten percent, an' I'd bet my life I increased its literacy rate by one hundred percent. They looked like homeless people standing around under an overpass to get out of the rain, which was coming down like a cow pissing on a flat rock."

Reverend Standish, who'd been listening intently, said, "This is a most interesting view into the creative process."

Bill looked incredulously at Reverend Standish. "Creative process?"

"One doesn't really think about signings and readings as being such an important part of getting a novel into the hands of its audience."

"Creative process? Audience? I manufacture books. One book every six months. And every fucking one that's been sold *I've* sold. If I don't sell 'em they sit in my publisher's basement until they get mildewed and he throws 'em out. There's your creative process."

"Most interesting. How many of these appearances do you make?"

"Damned if I know. I been in some of those bookstores more than the teenagers who work there. I tell Jeannie to schedule me and she schedules me. I'm on the road half the time flogging books."

"You know, I have this idea for a lawyer novel," Hymie interjected. "Something like Grisham's stuff, only better. You know—literary stuff. It's about this lawyer in Napa Valley who's got this successful practice in San Francisco and he's also this wine expert who travels to France every year to evaluate the new wines and writes a wine column in *The New York Times*, and he owns this upscale winery. One day when he's sailing his America's Cup challenge boat in the bay this guy in a speed boat comes racing by and peppers his sailboat with an AK-47 and—but I don't want to get into the plot right now. Let's just say it involves industrial espionage in the wine business. I was wondering if I should write a chapter before I send the idea to an agent. Or do you think I should just sketch the plot and have an agent sell it before I bother with the writing?"

"All those appearances—must take amazing stamina. When do you find time to write?" Reverend Standish murmured reverently.

Bill's white beard spread in a grin. "I'm writing right now. This stupid conversation's gonna be in my next book."

Reverend Standish nodded admiringly. "Sure, waste not, want not. Wow. I sure wish I had your determination. And talent, of course. I've been writing poems all my life. I guess I can say without boasting that I've even published a few. One's in the winter issue of *Practical American Poetry*, as a matter of fact. There's not much money in poetry, of course, but I always dreamed of being able to occupy all my time writing poems. Maybe if I had your determination—"

"You got a good day job," Bill said. "Keep it. Preaching pays a hell of a lot more than writing books—or driving a taxi, which is what I'd have to do if I gave up writing. Keep your job, cherish it. Consider yourself blessed. I gotta sell my books or we don't eat. Instead of writing, find something else to do with your life, something socially constructive. Like maybe pimping for your neighbor's teen-aged daughter, or robbing Seven-Elevens."

James smiled knowingly. "A lot of writers don't have to do all those signings."

"Which ones don't?" Bill challenged.

Morgan was not following the conversation very closely. His brain was clicking through a recap of his conversation with Shree. His irresolution had already gotten him into a pile of trouble. It appeared that their impromptu hot-tub liaison that afternoon had transmogrified his relationship with his sister-in-law into an affair. The word aspirated threateningly along the synapses of his brain. Affa-a-a-air.

And then he was aware that Shree had approached the group, that she had edged into the space between him and fat Jack. Morgan's heart ticked faster, and he felt his face warming and his groin tightening.

"Where you been?" Jack said placidly.

"Inside, to warm up." Addressing the group: "I don't know how you can stand it out here." She pulled an oversized cardigan closer about her. "But I can now, 'cause I found one of Morgan's sweaters in the closet." To Morgan: "Okay if I wear it?"

Unwilling to trust his voice, Morgan nodded.

"Wish we could do a tub. That'd warm me up."

Morgan's racing heart raced even faster and he was sure everyone could hear the pounding. And he fervently hoped no one agreed with her.

Fat Jack grinned. "She just discovered hot tubs. She'd live in one if she could."

"Norman Mailer, for one," James said. "And I'll bet Hemingway never did a signing."

"You a Mailer? A Hemingway?"

"Well, no," James allowed. "My stuff is more like Updike's—focus on the middle class, that sort of thing."

"We got a new Updike here, folks. Still writing his first novel and he's already Updike, ready to make a fortune explaining the middle class to the middle class."

"I finished it," James said. "I didn't want to say anything, because it would sound, you know, like boasting or something, and so I wanted to hold off until I get a contract. I sent it out to some agents weeks ago."

"You did?" Shree asked, even more incredulously. "You wrote a *book*? A whole book?"

James blushed, but looked pleased. "Yeah."

"What's it about?"

It was only then that Morgan, unsettled as he was by his mental recapitulation of his kitchen capitulation, recognized that his son had just announced that he'd finished the novel he had for three years claimed to be writing—which Morgan, for three years, had believed was simply another of his son's bullshit excuses for not studying enough to get decent grades.

"God!" Shree breathed. "What a talented family!"

"What about technical writing?" Morgan asked, before he realized that the others were not necessarily tuned to the logic underlying his words. Which was that if you're going to be a writer, the best kind of writer to be is the kind who earns money writing. And the only writers he knew who actually earned a decent living writing were the technical writers in the cubicles across the hall from his office. "Technical writers make a hell of a lot of money," he finished lamely.

"Whores," Bill sniffed. "Prostitutes."

"I got the idea when I was sailing in the bay a few weeks ago," Hymie said. "In an hour I had it all worked out in my head. Now all I got to do is write it."

❧

"Did you know he finished that book?" Morgan asked, when he and Jane were alone in the kitchen.

Jane smiled. "Not until this evening, though Lynn kind of hinted that he's done something important. I never thought he could do it. He was never a reader. Not an avid reader, which is what you think writers have to be, so I thought it was a phase, something he'd get through, like wanting to grow up and be a cowboy. But he did it. Actually did it. I'm very proud of him."

"He's gonna be a father in a few weeks, a father with no job and no money. He needs a job that pays money."

"Don't be so pessimistic."

Morgan filled his wine glass and raised it to his lips.

"He might sell it," Jane said.

"That takes a load off my mind."

"Here, take these out to the table, then come back and get the cheese plate. After that you can slice some of that Italian sausage."

Morgan carried the plate of vegetable dip and the basket of bread out the back door to the table, around which Lynn and Jeannie and Norma had gathered to graze. Morgan placed the food on the table and looked out into the yard, to announce that the food was ready. But the yard was empty. He went to the edge of the deck and sniffed the air. He returned to the kitchen.

"You've got to go out there and tell Jack to keep his pot in his pocket."

She put the knife down. "Oh, God. Where's Reverend Standish?"

"With Jack and Bill and Hymie and James, I suppose. The only place they can be is at the side of the garage."

"The salmon's in the oven. I can't leave it. You go."

"He listens to you, not me. They all do."

"Because of the way you talk to them."

"You always say that, and I don't know what the fuck you're talking about."

"Will you please not use that kind of language with me? It's abusive, it's a form of violence, an attack."

"Fucking right it is," Morgan said, as he turned and left the kitchen, walked past the table on the deck and down the two steps to the yard. He followed the brick walk and rounded the corner of the garage as Reverend Standish expelled a steam of smoke and passed the tiny brass pipe to James.

"Well, usually I don't care for poems," Bill said. "But I gotta admit that was a good one."

"Thank you very much," Reverend Standish said humbly. "Coming from a published writer, that means a lot."

James passed the pipe to Jack, who tapped the ash from its bowl and dropped it into his pocket.

"The food's ready," Morgan said. "Why don't we all go in and eat."

Reverend Standish grinned lopsidedly. "Morgan, this is some party. I haven't been to a party like this since I left the seminary. You have no idea how much I mess, I mean I miss, having artists around me. You're really lucky, you know. Such a talented family. Two novelists and a lawyer—one who's even writing a book. Wow."

"Dad is not so high on writers, are you, Dad?" James said dreamily.

Smiling woodenly, Morgan stepped aside and let the others pass.

&

Morgan glided, naked and noiseless, to the open window. The whine of the water-circulation motor was not loud enough to drown the words or the laughter coming from the deck below. He looked between the panels of the drapery down at the tub. Ten minutes before he had half-carried, half-dragged Jane up the stairs and dumped her on the bed, where she now snored. Shree and fat Jack had left the tub minutes before, dressed, and departed. Bill and Jeannie had gone home hours before, and James and Lynn had gone to bed after Reverend Standish departed.

Norma giggled. "Here?"

"Sure, why not?"

Norma squinted up at the deck light, above which Morgan lurked, naked and erect, behind a curtain. "They'll see us."

"Who cares." Hymie slid one arm round her shoulder and the other hand between her legs.

"Hey, stop that."

Crooning: "Hey-y-y, come on, you've been sending signals all night, telling me you're ready—and now I can feel you're ready."

"They'll see," she murmured again, and squirmed, but did not move away. Morgan watched them kiss and grope one another, and then Hymie said something to her and she giggled and both rose. He sat on the edge of the tub and leaned back on his extended arms and she put her face in his lap; and then Hymie sucked his breath and looked up at the window, grinning ferociously: "I'll bet he's watching right now."

Morgan did watch. For five minutes more, then jacked off as his wife snored; and though Norma and Hymie were still going at it, he came away from the window. At the side of the bed he cleaned himself and pulled the covers back and slid between the sheets and listened to the night noises of his inert wife.

ALLERGIES

Wilbert pointed the remote at the TV and punched a button. The screen flashed, and *The 700 Club*, which Sandra had been watching, was replaced by the emerald green of a baseball diamond. The lower-right corner of the screen showed an eight-to-zero score, not in favor of the Mariners.

"Shit, Jim Smith's pitchin' again," Wilbert said. "No wonder we're gettin' our asses kicked. I don't know why we don't trade the sonofabitch. Or send him down to Everett." He spoke conversationally, but Sandra knew he was talking to the TV, not to her. He almost never said anything to her—unless it was a demand or a complaint, such as a supper-time command for more fried potatoes, or an interrogation about why the fried potatoes were so greasy, or why they were so dry.

"Think I'll get a beer when this inning's over," he said to the TV. This, Sandra knew, was an instruction for her to bring him a beer. He regarded this circumspect mode of command as a liberal-minded concession to the modern age, wherein civilized people accepted the equality of men and women in all respects—except, of course, in abilities and roles; a rather optimistic world, he thought, the world he liked to think he inhabited; as opposed to, say, the darker worlds of Muslims and other lesser humans such as Africans and East Indians and Asians.

"I bought you some Bud Lite. You want that or the Miller's?"

"Bud."

Closing her Bible, which she'd picked up when he changed channels, she pushed herself up out of her recliner (the twin of his) and limped into the kitchen and opened the refrigerator. She limped back with the bottle, which she placed on Wilbert's side of the lamp table that separated the two recliners. Her limp came from a back injury she'd suffered several months before when she'd tried to move a box of Wilbert's engine parts, left over from the years when he was building drag racers, and for two decades refused to throw away, and which he'd left, for an unknown reason, in front of the freezer door.

He located the beer with a sidelong glance, picked it up, and brought it to his lips. He was already in a recumbent position—made necessary by the size of his gut—so he didn't need to even tip his head back to allow the beer to flow down his gullet; he merely brought it to his lips and tilted it until it poured into his mouth. He downed the beer in continuous, leisurely gulps, and put the empty bottle back where he got it. Belching, he gave her a compliment: "Bud's good. I'll get me another one when this inning's over."

She rose again and limped into the kitchen and got another bottle and placed it beside the empty on the table.

He was finishing the second beer when she murmured, "I went to the doctor's today."

He did not respond. When Sandra went to the doctor it was usually about problems that weren't really problems; she usually went about messy stuff that she could've avoided if she'd been careful—such as menstrual cramps and unpleasant discharges and stuff like that. So he wasn't very sympathetic.

"She said the reason I get the swelling was a allergy."

"Did you see that? Fuckin' idiot tried to grandstand a catch by slidin' under it, an' ended up with air. They need to trade that sonofabitch. Or send him down to Everett."

"Wilbert, the doctor said I got this allergy."

"Ten to nuthin'. That's our Mariners."

"Wilbert, I got this allergy."

"I heard ya. So what am I s'posed t'do about it? The doctor's the one who can fix it, not me."

She opened her Bible and started reading, and he watched the game. After another inning she closed the book and spoke again. "It's a serious allergy."

"Speak up. You're always mumblin'."

"It's um—it's—um—"

His attention span for Sandra's issues was very short: before she'd murmured the second "um" he was looking back at the TV.

"It's a penis allergy."

"Did you see that?" he asked the TV, incredulously. Then he glanced at her, frowning to demonstrate his annoyance at her helplessness. "Well, Jesus, what d'you expect? You must eat two pounds of the fuckin' things ever week. Jes' quit buyin' the stuff and maybe the allergy'll go away." He looked back at the TV, muttering, "Jesus. I never liked peanuts, anyway; not even peanut butter, so I don't see why you even buy the shit."

"It's not peanuts, Wilbert. It's *penis*. It's a penis allergy."

Engrossed as he was in the game, her words didn't register with him for half a minute. Then he looked at her again, with raised eyebrows.

"It's a—the doctor uh—she said—it's a—"

"A *penis* allergy? You don't even have a penis."

"No—it's not a allergy that penises *get*, it is a allergy *to* penises."

"You tellin' me you're allergic to my dick?"

"Well—umm. Yes."

He stared at her.

"She says it's why I get all puffy, an' have those palpitations, and the breathing problem. It's a allergy."

"Penis allergy? I never heard o' such a thing."

"Doctor Carter says it's pretty common. Only most women mistake it for something else wrong with them. But she says it's usually not something else. It's usually penis allergy."

∾

For a couple of weeks Wilbert was baffled about how to respond to Sandra's revelation. He took his cue, finally, from what he figured any real man would do. A real man would be outraged if his wife negligently got a penis allergy. And he was a real man. So there you are: he was outraged. Though, it has to be admitted, his outrage was a bit hemmed in by an ambivalence that stemmed from a nagging suspicion that maybe he wasn't really much of a real man, inasmuch as his diabetes and his inexorably ballooning belly had long ago combined to produce both a physical and a physiological impediment to the performance of his duty—the manly one. In fact, for several years his erections hardly got going before they wilted dismally, which so humiliated him—a man barely in his fifties—that he finally mustered the courage to tell *his* doctor, who got him started on those blue pills.

Naturally, she was contrite about the allergy. But contrite didn't do it for Wilbert, who, being a man of stern principles, did not forgive easily; particularly when there was advantage to be gained from unforgiveness. So he made sure she understood how hurt and angry he was about her betrayal. But even as he enjoyed his outrage, another dynamic was starting to develop. Percolating up from the cluttered recesses of his brain was a growing awareness that, upset as he was, he was also very relieved that her allergy had apparently rendered his penis—well, superfluous. In fact, he was hoping that her allergy had put that manly appendage into permanent retirement. In his portly condition, performing his duty, even with the help of the blue pills, was a big burden.

His wallet was also greatly relieved by Sandra's shocking betrayal: now he could stop buyin' those fuckin' pills. Jesus, the cost! In fact, one of his first thoughts, when Sandra informed him she had the penis allergy, was how to get his two hundred bucks out of the bottle of pills he'd picked up at the Safeway pharmacy just a month before, and still hadn't opened. He called the pharmacist and said he didn't need the pills after all and wanted to return them, but the pharmacist had cut him off impatiently, saying in her impenetrable Oriental-English that "something-something-something-something-something-something-something dwugs." Wilbert, taking that to mean he couldn't return unused drugs, didn't see why the fuck not, he hadn't even handled the fuckin' things, but by the time he got to the second f-word the pharmacist—a stupid fuckin' Vietnamese who didn't know her ass from a hole in the ground—had hung up on him. His next thought was maybe he could sell them on eBay. But eBay wouldn't even let him list the pills. After a few days of thinking about the blue pills he gave up on getting his money out of the damned things, and he put 'em away in the bathroom—which, he admitted reluctantly, was probably the smart thing to do anyway, inasmuch as it was possible that her penis allergy would go away as unpredictably as it came, in which case—well, he just might need to resume his manly duty, to prove he was capable of manly duty.

Though he enjoyed his outrage, he thought less often about her penis allergy as the weeks passed into months. But from time to time he could not help but note the beneficial changes wrought by the removal of the pressure of womanly duty from her and the removal of the pressure of manly duty from him. Their relationship had imperceptibly changed. The fullness of the change came to him one day as he was maneuvering his truck through the I-405 Kirkland crawl toward his last delivery (he did most of his thinking when he was behind the wheel) and it came to him that their life together was beginning to seem like a friendship. Well, not quite; in fact, he'd never thought of her as a friend, nor even as a companion. Nor had he ever regarded her as smart, clever, or good looking. He had always thought of her as a wife. When he met her, that was what he needed: a wife; so he'd married her. Her thick, squat body, her quiet demeanor, and her inexpressive face were irrelevant factors. Now, thirty-some years later, she was still all the things she once was, except one: she was no longer young. And like those *National Geographic* pictures of 1930s Russian peasant women, age had not so much changed her as plained her out. She was plain in every way it was possible to be plain: plain thinking, plain looking, plain cooking, plain talking. Not that he thought about it often, but when he did he always concluded she was the plainest, if not the boringest, person he knew. But now, instead of being bored and annoyed by the endless facets of her plainness, he found himself tolerating her almost as if she was one of his chums down at the VFW.

With the pressure of sexual expectations removed, Wilbert settled comfortably into his evolving relationship with her, and with the world. His nascent happiness would probably have grown and matured to contentment had a new VFW member not done him the service (or the disservice, depending on your point of view) of telling him that there is no such medical condition as penis allergy.

It happened like this. After the monthly meeting he'd joined three of his friends at their regular after-meeting meeting at Jack's Tavern to welcome a new member. The new guy, a rather young veteran of the '91 war in Iraq, said, when asked what he did for a living, that he was a medical technician in a Federal Way clinic. When the talk drifted to personal topics, the young man, feeling excluded, became quiet. Wilbert, generously seeking to bring the young fellow more actively into the conversation, recited a medical joke he'd made up. He mentioned that he knew a guy whose wife had a penis allergy, which of course meant the poor fucker couldn't fuck her anymore. He laughed uproariously. His pals, who'd heard his lame pun numerous times, smiled indulgently. The med tech smiled thinly and said, in a rather know-it-all voice, that if the guy believed that one, he was one extra-stupid schmuck. Because there's no such medical condition. Penis allergy was an inside joke in the medical profession about what women tell their husbands when they don't want to fuck them any more, and it nearly always means the wife wants to reserve her action for her boyfriend. Wilbert was stunned. He managed a sickly grin while the others laughed and slapped the table.

Sandra was in bed when he got home. He went right to the computer and Googled "penis allergy." Google returned several pages of penis enlargement sites and sex sites and sites advertising cures for things like jock itch. But he found nothing that would give any shred of medical legitimacy to the term penis allergy. When he finally fell into bed, at two o'clock, exhausted, he stared up into the darkness above the bed and listened to Sandra snoring, until it was time to get up and go to work.

෬

The next week was pure hell. He'd hardly gotten used to his new, relaxed, and expectation-free relationship with Sandra, when Sandra underwent another radical metamorphosis; this time into the inconceivable: a devious, cheating wife. Sandra, a cheating wife? Sandra, fucking someone else? It was impossible, outrageous, beyond imagination. Hell, he'd been screwing her for thirty-some years, and, to judge from the way she behaved while he huffed and puffed himself into a gargantuan sweat doing his manly duty, she was about as stimulated by it all as she was by ironing his work shirts. So now this sex kitten is fucking someone else? And out of choice? Yes, apparently; and that was the outrageous part: that she was *choosing* to screw this other guy. It wasn't like when he, Wilbert, screwed her—in that situation she was doing it because she had to. But these arcane distinctions meant nothing compared to the pain that Wilbert now suffered: his insides ached and churned with a humiliation beyond words, a pain beyond pain.

He began to feel as untethered from reality as a balloon drifting on the wind. He started doing irrational things. After she had her shower and got into her nightgown and robe and planted herself in front of the TV, where she read her Bible while he watched some sports event or a poker game, he'd get up and go to the bathroom and poke around in the dirty clothes hamper until he found her underwear. But he never found any evidence that she'd pulled them up after her boyfriend had delivered some of himself into her. And he took to calling the house in the middle of the day on some pretext or other—which he'd never done before—but he always found her there. In fact, his investigations confirmed that she almost never left the house except to go to the Friday Lunch Social over at the Federal Way Senior Center, or to do the weekly grocery shopping down at the Safeway and at Costco, and the

Hollywood Video for one of the girl flicks that she liked to watch on Saturday and Sunday nights after he went to bed.

Where could she have started her adultery? At the Senior Center? Wilbert could not see how that could be their meeting place. But what about the Wednesday night Bible study? Or maybe it was at the Sunday services, which she usually managed to attend both morning and evening. Or maybe she was sneaking out after he went to sleep. It was possible. He was in bed by nine on work nights and he slept like the dead, so she could go out for a couple of hours of coupling and he'd never know it. So he started noting the odometer reading on the minivan each evening before he went to bed, and in the mornings before he went to work. All of his detective work produced no information about her activities, except the obvious, which was the fact that she put very few miles on the minivan—and almost never during the evenings.

Thus it was that after a few weeks of clumsy investigation he knew nothing more than when he had begun. It seemed that the only real opportunities she had to meet up with someone were Sunday evenings, when she was supposedly in church, or on Wednesday evenings, when she supposedly went to Bible study. Fate seemed to be directing him, as it had directed generations of seekers, toward the church for an answer to his problem.

∾

To the pastor of Saving All Souls United Evangelical Church of Christ the Savior and Redeemer in Federal Way, his church was a business, and that business was salvation; which, he was fond of saying, was the most hopeful business in the world. Wilbert, on the other hand, held that it is a hopeless world we live in, where the good intentions of folks like Pastor

Johnson make everything worse than it needs to be. For that reason, he judged the pastor a fool, and he often iterated that sentiment to Sandra.

Thus, when he proposed to accompany her to Wednesday night Bible study, she looked shocked. In fact, she looked at him like maybe he'd slipped a cog. *Or*, he thought shrewdly, maybe she was scared he would learn even more about her adultery at her church.

Pastor Johnson greeted Sandra with a broad smile and a hug. He said some nice things about her as he held both her hands, and then realized that the fat man behind her was with her. He assumed he was her husband Wilbert, whom he'd never met. He thrust his hand at Wilbert. "So very nice to see you, Mr. Evans. Very nice, indeed. Welcome to our Wednesday night group." He seemed about to say more, but his restless eyes spotted a couple coming up the walk; and before Wilbert had a chance to respond, he gave a parting smile and clap on the back and was gone.

Sandra was limping away. Wilbert followed her past coat racks and through a wide double doorway into a large room arranged with several tables encircled by chairs. Every table was attended by at least one congregant, and several by as many as four. Most of them were women. Sandra took him to a table with two elderly men, whose conversation ended as she approached.

One of the men, a small slender fellow in a white shirt and bow tie, rose and pulled a chair out. "Good evening, Sandra," he said, with a nod that could almost be regarded as a bow. He looked at Wilbert. "And you must be Wilfred." He offered his hand. "Welcome to our table. I'm Harry Gordon and my friend here is Jim Savio."

Their greeting surprised Wilbert as much as the pastor's greeting. He had never seen anyone treat Sandra with such warmth, and even deference. But he reminded himself that he needed to stick to the purpose of this evening's investigation, which was to discover the identity of his adulterous rival. He gazed around the room and saw that he and Gordon and Savio were the only able-bodied men present. When he heard Harry Gordon say something to Sandra, the tone of his voice brought Wilbert's eyes back to the old fellow's face, which positively shone with enthusiasm and happiness. It came to him then, in something like an epiphany, that this puny little white-haired man, who couldn't weigh one-thirty sopping wet, whose grip felt as cool and soft as a woman's, was his rival. And, as if to confirm Wilbert's suspicion, Sandra actually smiled back at the little fellow. Wilbert could not remember when he last saw her smile directed *his* way.

Jim Savio spoke up. "Bet she keeps you on your toes, Wilfred. She does this group, even Pastor Johnson. She's one sharp cookie. In fact, she's the only reason I come—to hear her talk. Mostly these things are a waste of time, what with everyone always saying pretty much what they think God might like to hear."

Wilbert was puzzled. Was Savio poking fun at Sandra? He glanced at her, then Harry Gordon, then back at Savio.

"Jim's talking about the way Sandra challenges weak Christian values," Gordon said. He gestured to a chair. "Have a seat, Wilfred. The ladies will bring the tea out pretty soon, and then we'll start."

"Wilbert," Wilbert said.

"Beg pardon?" said Gordon.

"Name's Wilbert, not Wilfred."

"Yes, of course. Sorry about that. I get your named mixed up with a favorite poet of mine. Wilfred Owen. I suppose others do that as well, eh?"

Wilbert's eyes narrowed suspiciously. He did not understand what the little man said, but he thought it was probably ridicule.

Savio leaned toward Sandra with a mischievous smile. "And you still haven't convinced me that Jesus actually *meant* we're supposed to keep our faith private."

"You read Matthew six, five through seven?" Sandra asked.

"I did. And I still say that Jesus was talking about hypocrites who use prayer to show off. He wasn't saying that people are hypocrites *because* they pray."

"Jesus's words are very clear. Prayer should be private. When it becomes public it is no longer prayer, it is ritual. It's right there in black in white. He says it time and again—that ritual undermines his message, that ritual is the tool of hypocrites who seek to fool the people. Personally, I don't like any spoken public prayer, though I have to admit that you see it so much you just get used to it. But that don't make it right."

What the hell was she talkin' about? Though his confusion was making it hard for Wilbert to understand her, he was aware, for the first time, that he'd never actually seen his very religious wife in prayer. He had never given it a thought. But if he had thought about it, he'd have figured she just didn't want to bother with it—like him. Now it turns out that she's been prayin' all along, just not lettin' anyone see her do it. This revelation of still another complexity of Sandra's character deepened his confusion.

Pastor Johnson called the meeting to order and made some announcements about needing volunteers for this and that. After he read a couple of notices about special programs dealing with neighborhood issues, and answered a couple of questions, he announced the Biblical passage that would be the subject of next week's discussion. Then he read the passage assigned in the previous week and asked Sandra to start the discussion by commenting on it. *Sandra*? Why would anyone do that?

Pastor Johnson listened, acknowledged the wisdom of her words, but suggested that a more open interpretation might make it possible for Christians to demonstrate their fellowship by praying openly. This he thought important because it exposed the good news to those whose souls needing saving. When he finished speaking, the eyes in the room looked toward Sandra.

"I can't read the mind of Jesus, but I can read the words, and I am certain that I understand Matthew six, five through seven," Sandra said. "In fact, Jesus made all of his sayings clear and easy to understand. And we all know that Christians agree with them—except sometimes, when there's a cost to the belief. In this saying about prayer, just like Jesus's saying about money changers corrupting the temple, it is clear he is saying that when we mix our faith with the profane things of this world, like money and politics and personal power, we become hypocrites, and the only way to avoid that is to keep your prayer a private talk with God. Jesus is forbidding the use of prayer as a tool, because it makes us hypocrites. He used that word—hypocrites—a lot."

Pastor Johnson thanked Sandra for her stimulating and thoughtful analysis and looked around the room. "Now let's hear another point of view. How about you, Henrietta? What do you think Jesus meant?"

જી

As they drove home from the Wednesday night Bible study Wilbert still felt confused, in part because of Sandra's bizarre behavior, but also because he had not been able to develop incontrovertible proof that this Gordon fellow and

Sandra had a real bond. He just felt in his gut that they did. He brooded over the matter often in the following days, and found that, as the time passed, his uncertainty was evolving into certainty. Before long his doubts were gone. It was clear; he had found her lover out, and he was coming to the conclusion that he had to confront her. On Saturday night, after watching the Mariners get their asses kicked again, he got down to business. Focusing his attention on the problem of getting her to confess her adultery, he brought up the subject of the penis allergy.

"I suppose you still got that penis allergy," he said.

"I think so."

"You're not sure?"

"Well, I ain't been to the doctor for a while. But I still got the symptoms."

"Um." He nodded reflectively; it would take some subtlety to dig the truth out, but he was up to it. "Heard somethin' from a friend a mine down at Jack's Tavern the other day—a medical expert—who told me there's no such a thing as penis allergy. Says it's doctor talk about married women who save themselves for men they're not married to." He fell silent and looked over at her, to get her reaction.

Her reaction was shock, and then, as understanding came to her, a very red face. And Wilbert, with a sinking heart, thought, I'm right, I'm right, it's that Harry Gordon.

"I am—I have—I never been so—so ashamed. That you could believe such a thing of me—I don't have any words for it."

She closed her Bible, which she'd been reading during the game, and pushed herself up from her recliner. She limped across the living room.

This was not going exactly like Wilbert thought it would go. He had expected her to own up, through a flood of tears.

But she hadn't owned up. In fact, now it was her, the guilty one, doin' the accusin'—like he didn't even know what penis allergy really meant.

"Is it your friend Gordon?" he asked, determined to get this interrogation back on track.

She stopped in the bedroom doorway and faced him. "I have never given myself to any man but you."

He stared at her and she stared back at him, this time showing none of the humiliation he had seen on her face just seconds before. In fact, all he saw was an expression of disgust that he could not remember ever seeing on her face. In that instant, in another epiphany, he knew his first epiphany was dead wrong. His stomach flip-flopped inside him, and he wished he had not started this conversation. "You mean you—and—" He fell silent, as if he wanted her to speak.

She did not rescue him; she just stared accusingly at her false accuser. Her silence was very effective, but she was too much a woman to keep it going.

"The only time I ever seen Harry Gordon has been at the Friday lunch at the Senior Center and at the Wednesday night Bible study," she said. "Harry's wife is dead, and so is Jim's, so they spend a lot of time at the Senior Center. And at church. We sit together and talk about the Bible. Those two and the pastor are the only men I know who *like* to hear what I say. Who actually listen to me. You have managed to make that a ugly thing." She turned and went into the darkened bedroom and closed the door.

Wilbert—reclined in deference to his circumference— had been holding his head up to see her. A sudden weariness overtook him, and he let his head drop. He rolled his eyes over to the TV, which was now broadcasting the *Sports Wrap-up Hour.*

Jesus, the fucking energy it takes just to keep peace, he thought. Conversation with a couple of broken-down old men whose lives are so reduced they'll listen to anyone who tolerates their presence. Is that really all this thing amounts to? Apparently. And now she's pissed because he ain't like them? Wilbert snorted, signaling that his confidence had revived, and with it, his annoyance with the world. What does she expect, for Christ's sake? He's her husband, not her friend.

The Guy You Said Joyce is Fucking

Jack stopped at the doorway. Strewn across the floor were bra, wadded panty hose, shoes, blouses, skirts, flannel nightgown, a pair of jeans, a sweatshirt. A comforter and sheet were in a heap at the foot of the bed and towels trailed into the bathroom. Hanging over the side of the top drawer of the chest was another bra, and over the open closet door, Joyce's bathrobe drooped. He hoisted his bag to the bed, opened it, and began unpacking.

It was only in the dim hours of a United red-eye from Kansas City that he fully comprehended how stupid it had been to tell Freddie of his misgivings. Of all people, why Freddie? Jack didn't care about sparing his wife's feelings—not now, not after his discovery of her adultery—but he knew he would lose whatever control of the situation he possessed when the world knew about it—and the world *would* know as soon as Freddie could broadcast the news. Because information was all Freddie had to offer the world. In Jack's high-tech world, most people had skills to offer, but not Freddie. All Freddie had was a mouth, a curious mind, and a gift for trading information for advantage.

Jack went out of the bedroom and down the hall and into the long kitchen-family room, where he poured a glass of orange juice. He stood at the counter and drank it. He closed his eyes and rolled his shoulders to ease the stiffness that came from all those hours of meetings the day before, then the long

dinner with Garfield and his V.P.s, and the long wait at the
KC airport and, finally, the sleepless flight. He wanted sleep
very badly, but there would be no sleep today—not until
he repaired the damage. He picked up the telephone and
punched Freddie's number.

"Hello." In the background he heard a ripple of TV
laughter.

"Freddie, this is Jack. I—"

"Hey, man, glad you called. I heard something you need
to know."

"Listen, Freddie, I was calling to tell you that I was off
base the other night. What I told you—I feel like an idiot. I
was drunk, and pissed at Joyce about something, and I made
this stupid assumption—it was childish and stupid, and—"

"The guy's loaded—his fuckin' *house* takes up half an acre
on the water at Champagne Point. Five, six bedrooms at least;
beach; dock; boat. Probably two hundred feet of lakefront."

Silence. Then, "Who?"

"Arnold Keller, the guy you said Joyce is fucking."

"Jesus Christ, Freddie, I didn't say Joyce is *fucking* anyone.
All I said was she was acting distant, like she had—other
interests."

"Well, she has, man. And I found out who. It was easy,
man. All I did was go to her gym and park across the street
and wait for her to come out. I figured it had to be morning,
man. I mean, like what other time does she have? And if
it's morning, it's got to be the gym. Where they meet. Sure
enough, she comes out at six with this tall dude. They're both
in sweats, they get in separate cars, he drives off, she follows
him, and I follow her. They go to this apartment house a few
blocks away. They're in there for a half hour, she leaves, then
he leaves. I follow him home to forty-seven eleven Champagne
Point Drive. He's a widower, couple of kids. Boy eleven, girl

thirteen. A neighbor told me he moved in after he got money from an insurance settlement three years ago. Wife was killed when a tour bus pushed her car off a freeway ramp. Seems there's an old woman there all day—comes in the morning before he leaves and stays all day. A nanny, I guess."

"Freddie. I think you made a big mistake here—I think we better—"

"You want me to find out how often they're meeting at that apartment? Who's payin' the rent?"

"Fuck no," Jack blurted. "Jesus, Freddie, you got to put a lid on this. This is just a big misunderstanding, and if it gets out you're snooping for information on her, she'll—."

"Hey, man, I'm not a fucking gossip. I did this as a favor."

"Okay, Okay. Look, just keep this under your hat. This is just a big misunderstanding."

Jack stood at the counter for another minute, thinking about what Freddie had told him. He sighed, finally, and turned away. The damage was done. He went to the big double doors that opened onto the three-leveled deck, on the lower level of which was the hot tub, which overlooked the dock and sailboat. He thought about doing a tub, but decided he'd lie down for a while, first. He went back down the hall to the bedroom, took off his clothes, and crawled into bed. There, flat on his back, he stared at the ceiling until, after a half hour he gave up and rolled out of bed. He took the book he'd carried on the trip—*Giving Them Less And Making Them Think It's More: A Business Strategy for the 21st Century*—off the bed stand. Parker had bought copies for the Vice-President of Sales, the Vice-President of Manufacturing, the Vice-President of R&D, and for him, the Vice President of Engineering, saying he liked it so much that he wanted all of his senior managers to read it, and to be prepared to discuss its contents at the next Senior Staff meeting. Which was two days away.

A rich widower with two kids—Champagne Point—a nanny—five bedrooms—wife killed in an accident—insurance settlement—

All those bits of unwelcome information kept his mind in turmoil. His imagination, against his wishes, had developed a new and more interesting conception of Joyce's putative lover. He liked this one even less than the more imaginative one of his first impression. This new lover was sensitive, semi-tragic, semi-heroic; and far too sympathetic and easy to visualize as a male body superimposed on Joyce's female body. He shook his head, to drive the image out.

His instinct, which was all he had before Freddie's revelation, could be wrong, he knew. And his assumption of her activities on those several Saturday mornings mysteriously unaccounted for—she could have been at her office in Redmond—could also be wrong. Maybe she was going through a period when she was simply not horny. *That* seemed highly unlikely, however, given her undiminished appetite for the venal throughout their twenty-five years of marriage. Still, there could be any number of reasons for her present indifference.

But now Freddie's investigation had removed all doubt. He wondered: could Freddie be right?

Reading was impossible. He closed his book. Maybe a short drive, to get some air. Over to Champagne Point, for instance. It was only five miles. Might be interesting to see what the guy's house looks like.

℘

The road followed the left bank of a brushy ravine that meandered down the hill through a green tunnel of maple and alder. Jack was pleased by the rural feeling he got from swinging the Volvo through one woodsy curve after another, seeing no hint in the lush greenery on either side that he was snaking down the middle of a suburban park a quarter-mile wide and a mile long, with just enough trees and brush on both sides of the road to obscure clusters of upscale houses. The ravine gradually shallowed as he descended the hill toward the lake. When the trees fell away on either side, the road looped around to the south and into the open. With the lake to his right he followed the road past elegant, generously-spaced homes situated on the lakeshore. On his left was a tree-covered slope and equally elegant houses. He saw an address on a big two-story Georgian brick set back from a sandy beach: forty-six forty-one. He drove on.

Forty-seven eleven: the big brass numbers gleamed on the gray gabled wall above three garage doors. He pulled the car to the side of the road, along a low split-rail fence, and looked at the house. Above the numbers was white facia and a shake roof. To the left of the rambling structure the branches of a willow swept down into a surrounding bed of gravel and profusely flowering gardens. To the right of the house a bright green lawn sloped to a white beach and a dock, against which a sailboat swayed, its cockpit covered in pristine white. Jack observed all of this appreciatively: the contrast, in texture and color, of garden and gravel and lawn; the elegance of gray and white house beneath a roof of weathered cedar; the sensual contrast of green lawn and blue-green lake, separated by the white of boat and beach. The parts so pleasingly balanced they could have been composed by a fastidious artist. Was all this Arnold's work?

Jack sensed the presence of another. He looked up at the rearview mirror and saw eyes behind a windshield staring back at him. Then the face moved, and in the outside mirror Jack saw the door of the white Lexus swing open, and a thickly muscled chest in a tight T-shirt came into view beneath a crewcut head. Arnold Schwartzeneger, Jack couldn't help thinking.

Arnold approached, placed his meaty hands on the roof of Jack's car, and leaned his craggy head down between ham-like arms. "Anything I can do for you?" he asked in a rumbly voice.

Jack's heart was racing. He looked up at Arnold. "No," he squeaked, "no thanks. Just looking at the neighborhood."

"You were looking at my house. Makes me wonder for what purpose."

"Actually, I wasn't—not at your house, I mean. I was admiring your gardens. I often drive through nice neighbor-hoods—like this—to get gardening ideas." (Silence from Arnold.) "And yours— your gardens—caught my eye. When I see gardens as nice as these I just have to stop and look." Trying for a disarming smile, he achieved a pasted-on, guilty-looking grin.

Arnold did not smile. "What's your name?"

This was the question Jack had hoped Arnold would not ask.

"It's wonderful the way you developed the area around the willow. It's a perfect solution to problem trees like willows. They're so messy. How do you get the debris out of the gravel? Blower?"

Arnold studied Jack's face for several seconds, Then, still unsmiling: "The gardener does it." He folded muscular fore-arms across his chest. "What is your—"

"He certainly does a fine job. I have a big hemlock that drops so much trash that nothing grows under it. You wouldn't believe the tonnage big hemlocks drop. Trees like that also suck all the moisture out of the ground, you know, so even grass hasn't a chance. What you've done here—all that gravel—it's the perfect solution. Another thing that I admire very much is the health of the grass, this close to the lake. How does your gardener achieve that? Did he put drain tiles in? Of course up the hill where I live we don't have any drainage problem, but here—"

Arnold stepped back and made a movement of his head, which Jack took to be a command to move on. His face still twisted in a guilty grin, Jack fumbled with the keys, got the Volvo started, and sped off. He glanced up in the rearview mirror and saw that Arnold stood in front of his white Lexus, watching him.

೨

Joyce was holding a portable telephone to her ear with one hand and a shot glass of tequila in the other. Before her on the table was a saucer of salt and quarters of lime. She looked up at him and circled her mouth in a kiss. She continued talking as Jack came out on the deck and leaned down and put his lips to the cheek she offered.

"You need a change of environment," she said into the handset. She listened for a few seconds, then spoke again: "I know, but this is more important than a job."

Jack had started back into the kitchen to get a glass of orange juice, but he stopped and turned and looked at her with eyebrows arched. "Are you talking to Dan?"

She ignored him.

"Is that Dan?" he asked again.

Still ignoring him, Joyce cooed into the handset, "Sweetie, don't worry, it'll be okay."

"It *is* Dan."

"We have all the room in the world. You just need some time to kick back and not even think about it for a while. It'll all work out. You'll see."

"*What'll* work out? He's talking about quitting that job, isn't he."

"Well, she's right," Joyce said to the handset.

"Who's right? Right about what?" Jack waited, hands on hips.

"Promise?" she asked the handset.

"Promise what?"

"Okay, sweetie." As Joyce pushed the off button and placed the handset on the glass table, she looked coldly up at Jack. "I wish you wouldn't do that. I cannot carry on two conversations at one time. It's distracting and it's rude."

"It *was* Dan. And if I'm not mistaken, I heard you encouraging him to quit his job again and come whining home."

She glared at him, her lack of response telling him that that was, indeed, what he'd just heard.

"What's he complaining about now? They asking him to put in forty hours every week? It is too much for him?"

She stared coldly at him for several seconds, but her anger failed her. She looked away. "It seems Cindy has left him. And he's completely freaked out. It appears that he's behaving—rather—well, he's not very stable. And his boss has told him to take two weeks off and get his life together. He's afraid he's going to be fired."

"I *knew* it was gonna happen. I fucking *knew* it was going to happen when he and that creature got a place together. Is he back on pot?"

❧

Jack draped his trousers on the deck chair, then stepped out of his boxer shorts, which he folded and placed on the trousers. He hung his shirt on the back of the chair, then sat on the edge of the hot tub, swung his legs in, and slowly lowered his feet, then his calves, into the steaming water.

Joyce—who always disrobed by simply stepping out of whatever she was wearing—had dropped skirt, panties, blouse, and bra in a heap and was already immersed to her neck in the steaming water.

Jack lowered himself until he was sitting chest-deep in the hot water.

"You were right about the umbrellas," Joyce said, with an overdrawn sexual suggestiveness that Jack saw as obviously intended to distract him from the now-pressing topic of their son's newest life crisis. "Makes it so much more intimate."

The suggestion of sexual encounter, which was packaged in her coyness, did not soothe Jack's irritability. Jack had nursed his anger through dinner, and still clung to it, if for no other reason than he needed the energy of anger to keep him going under a growing weight of exhaustion and too many glasses of shiraz. He had reason for anger. He still could not believe he'd actually heard his irresponsible wife encouraging their irresponsible son to his greatest irresponsibility yet—throwing away the only fucking job he'd ever gotten on his own to come home and brood about the best luck he'd ever have, which was Cindy's evident desertion. All of Jack's effort, all the progress he'd made in months of alternately hectoring his son and pleading with him to stick it out with his job, were all but destroyed by a five-minute conversation with his mother.

The upper part of her body emerged from the water as she stood. "The effect of the umbrellas is quite exotic against the night sky. So big and red, and so perfectly placed."

Water gleamed on her breasts and belly. She brought her tequila to her lips, sipped, and picked a piece of lime from the saucer on the hot tub wall. She looked down at him. "We can do anything we want in the tub now, and no one can see." She lowered her face to his and delivered an open-mouthed kiss. This caught him by surprise; but he responded. After a few seconds she broke off, straightened, sipped once again, and lowered herself back into her sitting position, with water lapping at her chin.

"Lying in bed all alone last night, I thought about you," she said. "And today. About how we've let things get in the way."

We? We've let things get in the way? he almost asked—but didn't, because the kiss had made him think maybe it *was* possible that a fuck was lurking somewhere in this exchange. Her voice had that internal thickness that he'd once associated with sexual receptiveness—but which in recent years had come to suggest one drink too many of Don Julio's fine tequila. He could not tell which condition prevailed now, for she'd had a shot glass and lime in her hands all evening. Nevertheless, his heart quickened and he felt the lightness that comes with sexual anticipation.

"I love you," she said.

Her words, so unexpected, so simple, overwhelmed his irritability. A happy lassitude flowed warmly through him, defeating his suspicion. "Then let's make love," he croaked urgently. "Right now." He didn't say *before it's too late, before I pass out from exhaustion.*

She smiled teasingly over the lip of the glass. "Now? Here?" She sipped the drink.

"Yes, right now, right here."

"Fucking in a hot tub can kill you," she murmured, putting the glass aside. "And you're so tired. But I'll chance it if you will." She slid through the water and, folding her knees under her opened thighs, floated onto his lap. She put her hands between his legs teasingly and delivered another wet kiss. His hands roamed down her back and into the crease that separated her buttocks. She closed her eyes.

"Hey, what the fuck's goin' on out there?"

Joyce jerked wildly, with a look of panic; but for only half a second—the time it took to recognize Freddie's voice. Rolling her eyes, she sighed and sank back into the water, to her neck, as Jack, too dulled by exhaustion to be surprised, turned and looked. From behind Freddie, Wanda appeared, her eyes merry with the laughter she was suppressing.

"I told you we shouldn't 've come in," she said, her scolding voice at odds with her evident enjoyment of the situation.

"Well, shit, they should lock the fuckin' door if they don't want people comin' in," Freddie boomed as he came to the side of the tub. "Don't get up, we only come to get a couple of boxes out of the garage."

Wanda was lankier than Jack remembered, and taller. And while her tiny flat nose was not her most attractive feature, neither was it the unattractive blemish he had seen the first time they met—which was a week or so after she and Freddie came back, married, from Reno. As a matter of fact, in this light, at this moment, her pert little nose—flat as it was—was positively charming. Or maybe it was the intrusiveness of her gaze, which held Jack's for several seconds, which made her seem more interesting. He watched her eyes move from his face to his chest and through the clear water over his belly and into the blond pubic patch in which his manhood lurked, reminding him, as he followed her gaze with his own eyes, of a turtle sticking its head out of its shell. Her inspection was pleasantly physical. And he did not mind it; in fact, he enabled it a bit by letting his torso float a little higher in the water.

Joyce, in a voice thickened by tequila, said: "You know where the boxes are, Freddie, just get what you need."

"We're really sorry," Wanda said, looking up from her inspection of Jack to smile at Joyce.

"What boxes?" Jack said as Freddie disappeared into the kitchen.

"Freddie stored some boxes in the garage," Joyce said.

"To make room for his work table and stuff," Wanda offered, once again eyeing Jack's chest and belly.

Jack slid forward just a little, to accommodate her eyes—aware that the sensation emanating from his lower torso indicated that the turtle was venturing forth.

"Can you believe I've never even been in a hot tub?" Wanda said, noting Jack's offering.

"No kidding," Joyce said thickly. Jack heard the edginess that had come into her voice. Evidently she had noticed Wanda noticing Jack's offering. "I would have guessed that you've spent many an evening in a hot tub."

That edginess Jack heard in her voice was the truest thing he'd heard from her all evening. She had definitely noticed the nascent communication between Wanda and him, which, based as it was on her observation of his dick, was enough to piss her off. Which rather pleased Jack.

Apparently unaware of Joyce's irony, Wanda said, "I always wanted to try it, but never had the opportunity."

Through the haze of his exhaustion Jack realized that Joyce had decided he was territory she would defend: a pleasing turn of events. "You can join us, if you like," he said, to keep the enjoyable tension going. And then he remembered that by inviting Wanda into his hot tub he was also inviting Freddie. And probably foregoing his piece of Joyce's ass. Shit. He began a mumbled retraction of the invitation with phrasing that was intended to move it from the *now* to an uncertain time in the future—phrases like "sometime," or "the next time you walk in on us doing a tub" came to mind. But it was too late: Wanda got busy getting her *I Luv Reno* T-shirt up over her face and simply ignored his muttered retraction. In a flash she was out of her bra and pushing her jeans and panties down over her knees. In his hallucinatory state the revelation of her willowy white nakedness bending and turning through the movements of disrobing and entering the hot tub had the grace of an elegantly slow-motion dance—a kind of hillbilly kabuki. Mesmerized, he forgot all about dissuasion. She lifted her left leg—with about as much immodesty as it was possible to display while still in an upright position—and slid one foot into the water until she was straddling the hot tub wall, facing Jack. She paused, perhaps to reward him for his generosity by permitting his inspection of, well, *her*, then shifted her weight to the inside leg, and gracefully brought the outside leg in. Jack observed this dance from a distance of some twenty inches. She lowered herself to a sitting position, allowing the water to come up to her breasts.

She sighed and closed her eyes, murmuring, "Oh, I had no idea it could be this good. It's so—so—geez, taking a bath with a man you don't even know is so *weird*, but it's like, exciting, too. You know?" She smiled at Jack. "It's hard to believe this is only the third time we've ever met."

"Never taken a bath with a strange man before?" Joyce said, with a stiff smile. "I find that hard to believe."

Wanda smiled innocently. "If I had a hot tub I'd do it every night." Her gaze slid over to meet Jack's. "I'll bet you do it every night, don't you, Jack?"

Jack knew he was hallucinating when he observed her breasts—well, *floating*. The coquettish, white demi-globes topped by tiny brown demi-globes of nipple, fixed to her body—and yet apparently floating slowly toward him. Her last sentence belatedly registered in his consciousness: ". . . bet you do it every night. . . ." Even in his condition of near collapse, he knew that was bullshit.

"Not even close," he said hoarsely. "Joyce doesn't like to do it with *me* any more. I think she's savin' it for Arnold."

The silence that followed told him he might've said something wrong. Before he could figure out what it was, a loud metallic *BANG!* sounded from the kitchen door.

Wanda looked around. "What was that?"

Jack looked dazedly from Wanda to Joyce, who pushed herself to her feet, leaned out of the tub, and got a towel, which she wrapped round her torso as she climbed out.

"Freddie," she said, as if that explained everything.

At that moment Freddie came into the kitchen. "It's all right," he called. "Took a little fall is all it was. But I'm okay—landed on the Volvo." He saw Wanda looking over her shoulder at him as he came out onto the deck. "You little devil! Outta my sight for ten seconds and you've got your clothes off."

"Are you hurt, sweetie?"

"Naw. Landed on my back, on the hood of the Volvo. It gives pretty good."

Jack dimly perceived Freddie had said something disagreeable about his Volvo. "What? What about the Volvo?"

"It feels so good, Freddie, can we get one? Please?"

Joyce dropped her towel and climbed—a bit unsteadily— back into the hot tub.

"One what?" Jack asked dazedly.

"Now where the hell we gonna put a hot tub?" Freddie said, as he kicked off his shoes. "The livin' room?"

Jack, still worried by something Freddie had said—oh, fuck yes, about Arnold; and about his Volvo—watched Freddie peel his shirt and drop his pants and underwear. And then Jack's fragmentary thoughts about the Volvo evaporated. His mind—now in that near-implosive stage that accompanies complete exhaustion—had abandoned logic and reason, and probably any ability to make sensible observations. Freddie's top-to-bottom hairiness he believed because it was right there in front of him to see and because it fit with his conception of Freddie as a primitive creature. But the part of Freddie hanging out of the mat of hair below his washboard belly—*that* could not be real, except perhaps attached to the belly of a horse. It had to be hallucination. He closed his eyes to give his brain a chance to clear this obvious error of perception: his wife's freaky, freakin' cousin Freddie could not possibly possess the poundage that he'd just dragged ponderously over the hot tub wall as he stepped into the water. Jack opened his eyes and saw that he was not hallucinating. And he also saw that there was no justice in the world, no equity among men, no fairness in the distribution of wealth. But he also knew that no revolution could redress this unfairness; that the inequity he observed was as immutable as the past. He remembered Wanda's eyes searching for him down through the water and understood her curiosity: to her his organ must seem freakish; no more than a miniature model of Freddie's gargantuan endowment. He blushed.

"Did Wanda show you her new earrings?" Freddie asked. "Diamonds. Cost me three and a quarter, but she's worth it." Freddie leaned toward Wanda and put his hand on the inside of her thigh, drawing her close.

Wanda smiled, and, pushing her hair away from her ears, turned her head first to one side, then the other to display the adornment in her ear lobes. "He comes home and says he has something to show me, and when he pulled this box out of his pocket and give it to me and I saw what was inside I almost wet my pants."

Freddie was smiling at Jack. "You know, most of the time you're so fuckin' uptight. I never told you how much I resent the way you're always lookin' down on me 'cause I sell used cars and you're this hotshot V.P. of something or other. But tonight you seem different. It's like something has made you more *likeable*—you know?"

When Jack looked vaguely confused by this revelation, Freddie raised a hand. "It's okay, I could care less what you think a me. But I bet a little pot once in a while would be a great help to your personality."

"He doesn't need any pot," Joyce said. "He's exhausted. From a trip. But I need another drink. And who the hell is Arnold, anyway?"

"What're you drinkin'?" Freddie asked.

"Don Julio."

"Say no more," Freddie said, "I could use one, too." He stood, confronting Jack once more with nature's bounteous inequity.

"It's on the counter," Joyce said as Freddie hoisted one leg, then the other, out of the tub.

Jack closed his eyes. He heard Wanda say something, then Joyce's response, then Wanda's sing-song giggle, then cheerful laughter from the both of them. Apparently they'd put aside the strain that had been there just moments before: perhaps he wasn't worthy of feminine rivalry.

When he opened his eyes again, with a jerk of his head, he was sputtering and water was dripping from his face. He saw that Freddie was sitting opposite him once again, sucking now on his little brass pipe; that Joyce sat naked on the hot tub wall, elbows on knees, feet in the water, head down, eyes closed; and Wanda was leaning against Freddie with one hand in his lap looking dreamy-eyed. Freddie passed the pipe to Wanda, who took it with her free hand and drew smoke into her lungs. Noticing that Jack's eyes were open, she offered the pipe. He studied it for several seconds, then, as if under compulsion, reached across the space between them and took the pipe and drew smoke into his mouth. He held it there for a few seconds, intrigued by its strange, skunky tanginess, then inhaled like it was the pure air of a country evening. It felt like he'd been speared right in the middle of his chest.

❧

"We gotta dry him off a little. He'll get the bed all wet and catch a cold."

"Who fucking cares? Jesus, you'd think people like this would have it together. Look at 'em. Fuckin' drunks. If we hadn't showed up they'd both've drownded."

"He's not drunk. Just a little too much to drink is all. And too much pot—which you gave him."

"Which *you* gave him. What a pussy. It was only one hit."

"I'll get a towel."

"Shit. This is disgusting."

Jack felt the towel moving over his back, down each of his legs, his arms, over his chest and belly, and then down between his legs, accompanied by Freddie's snarl: "Gawddamnit, keep your fuckin' hands off his cock! Jesus!" And Wanda, giggling: "I'm just drying him off. Besides, his little dick is so cute." Jack tried to tell them his dick was not cute, it was a brutal, murderous, punishment machine. But nothing came from his mouth except a bit of drool. What are they doing with those fucking rags? He was perfectly capable of drying himself, even if he could not command his eyelids or his tongue. Nor his arms apparently, for when he tried to push free of Freddie's grasp he found his limbs had mutinied and joined the enemy.

And then he was on his back with the gentle weight of the comforter anchoring him to the bed. He succumbed.

"What about Joyce."

"Fuck her. I'm not dryin' off another body."

"She can't stay on the sofa."

"Why not?"

"She'll freeze."

"Find her a blanket."

Which was the last thing Jack heard until he looked up, through a cloud of pain, at Joyce nakedly berating him for sleeping on her side of the bed. He rolled over to his side and was instantly asleep once again.

EDNA'S MISSION

Reverend Wimmer hoped that Edna Snodgrass's visit had nothing to do with the gossip that was going around about her mother-in-law and Roy Gunterson. An adulterous relationship between a seventy-five-year-old widower and the wife of his demented best friend and neighbor, was as ridiculous as it was improbable. But Reverend Wimmer had a lot of experience ministering to injuries that God's children inflicted upon one another, so in these matters he regarded the improbable as quite probable.

"I need to talk to you," Edna Snodgrass said, "about what God has told me to do."

Reverend Wimmer's eyes narrowed. When one of his flock talked about what God told him or her to do it was a sure sign somebody was cooking up something wacky. And probably violent. He stood in the entry hall, pipe in one hand, a piece of paper in the other, while he cast about for a civil way to get rid of her. Which was a mistake, for she perceived his hesitation as an invitation to continue. She edged around him and into the tiny office just off the entry hall. She sat down in a straight-backed chair before his desk and clasped her hands in her lap, ready to talk about what God had said to her. The air was close, warm, and stinking of rancid pipes and stale tobacco smoke.

He followed apprehensively, slid behind his desk, and waited. A goose-necked lamp focused its light on the clutter of papers before him—fragments of old sermons, which it was his habit to cut and paste into new sermons.

"What it is, is this. Mom—not *my* mom, she'd never—it's George's mom—she's—see, she and—see, Roy Gunterson and her—" Edna Snodgrass stammered and mumbled and finally stopped, her face aflame, unable to say such ugly words to her minister. As a matter of fact, she couldn't bring herself to say *those* ugly words to anyone, not even to George. Even when she tried telling her best friend Stella, down at the Safeway deli, she couldn't actually *say* it.

While she tried to communicate the terrible thing to Reverend Wimmer, without actually talking about it, he tried to think of a way of getting her out of his house before she managed to communicate it to him, because that act would involve him in it.

Edna Snodgrass saw that he wasn't reading her mind, like she had hoped. She drew a deep breath and began again. "You know Roy Gunterson? The big, tall old man with the purple nose? That sits in the back? And doesn't come very often?"

Reverend Wimmer nodded cautiously. He had seen him, though he'd never talked to him.

"Well, it's them." Edna Snodgrass leaned back and crossed her arms over her ample breasts and waited for Reverend Wimmer to take the ball.

Silence.

"So I didn't know what to do," she said, when she saw Reverend Wimmer wasn't taking the ball. "You know—about it. Until God told me, is what I mean. Which is what I should tell you about, I guess."

Reverend Wimmer didn't want to know what God told her.

"Mainly because of Harry."

Harry?

Edna sighed. "Poor man. Harry doesn't know a thing about it. He's happy as a clam just watchin' the TV. That's all he wants. He's not with us very much any more."

Oh, Harry! Edna's father-in-law. Reverend Wimmer poked around in the papers on his desk for his pipe until he discovered he had it in his hand.

"God told me that the only way Harry's gonna be saved is for him to get that brain surgery the doctors want to give him. So guess what Edith's *not* gonna do?"

Reverend Wimmer didn't want to know.

She went on as if he'd guessed and missed. "She's not gonna let him have that brain surgery, that's what she's not gonna do. She says it's because it'd be too hard on him, that he might die, but that ain't the reason. God told me the reason is, is that she doesn't want him to be able to see how she's—how that Roy Gunterson and her—well, you know."

Reverend Wimmer fidgeted with his pipe and wished the phone would ring.

"'Course she never actually *told* me, not in so many words, that she's not gonna make Harry get that surgery, but it's as obvious as the nose on your face. So after God told me *he* wants Harry to have that surgery, so he can be a man and take charge of his life—*and* take charge of his wife, like a man's *supposed* to do—I knew God was telling me I got to be the one to do it."

Reverend Wimmer had never in his whole life heard God say a single word. Not one. So he was more than a little skeptical when people talked about God talking to them. It was his experience that people who talked about God talking to them were about to cause a lot of pain and trouble for someone and were setting God up to take the fall for it. He tamped tobacco into the bowl of his pipe, more nervous now, because he was thinking that if he got involved in this adultery it might be *him* the trouble was heading for.

"What I'm thinkin' of doing is this. I'm thinkin' I need to go and tell Edith to let the doctors give him that surgery."

Reverend Wimmer lit his pipe and blew a cloud of blue smoke into the air above the desk. Well. This might not be as bad as he'd first thought. At least God hadn't told her to murder Roy Gunterson.

"Maybe she'll let the doctors give him the operation he needs. I was wonderin' if it's the right thing to do. Should I go and talk to her?"

Reverend Wimmer was relieved. He tamped and lit his pipe again, thinking that this little episode of familial dysfunction was more or less harmless. He didn't detect any of the hatred and violence that he usually saw when adultery cropped up in his congregation.

"I don't see no other way," Edna Snodgrass continued.

Reverend Wimmer rolled his eyes thoughtfully up, drew on his pipe, and expelled a big cloud of blue smoke.

"So. You *do* think I ought to just take the bull by the horns and do it? God didn't say much about that part of it. Just said I'm supposed to do something about it."

He ran a pipe cleaner through the bit of his pipe, stuck the pipe back in his mouth, and wrinkled his brow thoughtfully.

"Yes, I agree," she murmured. "I will do it. Thank you for your advice."

❧

"No way, Jose," George said emphatically.

Edna Snodgrass put her hands on her hips. "Well, it's *your* mom and dad involved in this, not mine."

"I said I ain't goin'. An' I'm not gonna talk about it, neither, or listen to you talk about it, so you might as well just shut up."

She sniffed. "*You* were the one tellin' your mom and ever body else, all year long, ever time you had the chance, that Dad *had* to have this surgery. *Had* to have it. Now you won't even talk about it."

"Get out o' the fuckin' way."

"You're just gonna sit there in front of that TV and let your dad—well, just be made a fool of like by your mom and that Roy?"

"Yes, I am. 'Cause it's none o' my fuckin' business. Now get out o' the way. I'm busy trying to watch—shit, now what the hell happened? Washington had the fuckin' ball just a minute ago and now look, the Ducks got it on the five. Shit."

The telephone rang. Edna Snodgrass went to the telephone stand, which was the company headquarters of Plumbing Concepts. She made a motion, which he ignored, for him to turn the volume down, then picked up the telephone handset.

"Plumbing Concepts," she announced. She listened for a few seconds, glanced at George, and said, "Yes, we do that all the time. No, there's no extra charge for Saturday." She scribbled something on a piece of paper. "Three's fine. We'll have one of our trucks there at three. Thank you."

She returned to her position between George and the TV, which caused him to have to lean off to the side to look around her again.

"You got a job up on the plateau."

He looked up at her. "The Huskies are playin'."

"The lady wants you there at three."

"Shit. You did that just to ruin my game."

"I'm going over to talk to your mom. Then I'm goin' to work. I won't be home 'til seven."

"What about supper? Who's gonna fix supper?"

"I'll bring some fried chicken from the deli when my shift's over."

℘

Edna Snodgrass got out of the car and smoothed her Safeway apron down over her belly. She looked up at the house and was certain she saw Roy's big purple nose in the front window. As she walked up the driveway she heard the back door slam. It *was* Roy, she thought contemptuously, and now he's high-tailin' it for home. The image of him fleeing from the embarrassment of her witness to his adultery made her feel powerful. She couldn't help liking the feeling, though she didn't believe it was right for a Christian woman to feel that way. Her being a woman and all, an' Roy bein' a man. She was more used to, and comfortable with, God's natural order.

She went around to the back door, tapped, and waited. Edith's face appeared in the window, then the door opened and Edith stepped back and permitted her daughter-in-law to enter.

"I was just about to make some coffee," Edith said coolly. "Please have a seat."

Talking to me like I'm some stranger she just met, Edna Snodgrass thought. It was what she expected. They'd spoken only twice since she had first hinted to her mother-in-law that she knew about the carrying on with Roy, and their conversation had been short and cool. Edna went to the kitchen table and pulled out a chair and sat and clasped her hands around her purse and while she waited to see what would happen next, watched Edith pour water into the coffee maker, slide the filter tray out, add a filter and some coffee, then slide the tray back in.

"Nice of you to drop by," Edith said, a bit too formally. "How's my son?"

"He's fine. He's on a job right now, up on the plateau."

"Um."

Silence while they listened to the coffeemaker burp and gurgle.

"How's Harry."

"Same as always. He's in the livin' room, watchin' TV."

"Um."

The coffee maker gurgled and burped more urgently, and the smell of fresh coffee floated through the air. Edith got up and went to the cabinet and got cups and a plate of cookies and brought them to the table with a carton of milk and a bowl of sugar. She poured the coffee and resumed her seat.

Edna Snodgrass drew a deep breath. It was time to do what God had told her. "How's Roy?" she asked, to introduce the subject.

Edith stirred sugar and milk into her coffee. "I suppose he's all right," she said.

Edna Snodgrass picked up an oatmeal cookie and took a bite. It was a very good cookie. Edith's cookies were the envy of every woman who'd ever tried one. She ate the rest of it and got another.

Crumbs popped out of her mouth as she mumbled: "I come to find out what you're gonna do about Harry."

Edith paled. She had been asking herself that painful question continuously for a year; and the question had become even more painful now that Roy was also asking it. But it had never been as painful as at that moment, when her daughter-in-law asked it. Edna had stumbled into the moment when the pressures had reached the maximum levels, when she could not accept even the smallest increment of additional pressure. The innocuous question, meant to be an opening to a discussion of what God wanted, stabbed her like a spear.

Edna dipped her second cookie in her coffee, and ate it while she watched Edith struggle for composure.

"I don't know—I been thinking—" Edith blinked rapidly at the tears welling in her eyes. Her voice broke, her words softened and trailed off into silence. She watched her daughter-in-law eating cookies as cool as you please while the ground heaved, while the world came unstuck, came flying apart, and accusation became judgment and judgment became sentence and sentence became execution. She burst into tears.

Edna stuck the rest of a cookie into her mouth, brushed the crumbs from her bodice and lap, and rose and went to her sobbing mother-in-law and leaned over and hugged her and said, through the little crumbs of cookie that jumped out of her mouth: "It's okay, Mom, it's gonna be fine, you'll see. God's looking out for all of us."

Harry heard the wailing and sobbing, but he was urgently busy watching a movie that he knew he'd watched dozens of times, but was always frustratingly new. He had no idea how it was going to turn out, as he had no idea how it had started out, but he wasn't about to give up—and he sure as hell wasn't going to be distracted by the ruckus. At that moment the two women, tearing their hair like the women of Troy, burst out of the kitchen and grabbed him in their arms and pressed their fat, soft breasts against him in front and back and pushed their wet faces into his neck.

"Don't worry, Dad, it's gonna be okay," Edna sobbed.

Harry's expression took on a look of exasperation and he raised his head a little so he could look down over Edna's head at the TV screen. The scene was so familiar, and yet it was all so new.

WINNER

When you've been married twenty years you know the appetites of your mate. When she's horny, you know it, and when she's not, you know that, too; and it doesn't take a PhD in psychology to figure out *why* she's not, *when* she's not. Carrie has never been hard to read. She's always had a healthy appetite for sex, and she's always expressed it as an expectation. Until five months ago.

Such are George's ruminations as he stares out the window behind his desk at a low brooding sky that perfectly matches his low brooding mood. He thinks about the changes in his life that have been brought about by changes in his wife. She's as healthy today as she's ever been; and there are no problems at work. In fact, she was recently promoted to senior vice president, evidence she is as aggressively ambitious now as she ever was.

So what *has* changed in Carrie's life that has caused her affections for him to wane? He knows, of course, though he would rather continue looking for some reason less fatal to their marriage. In fact, for months he has pulled back from the truth that her focus on him began to wane about the time the new couple moved into the house at the end of the cul-de-sac: Endicott, a brash and athletic lawyer pushing fifty-five, and Susan, a talkative, bookish tech writer pushing thirty.

He has no hard evidence that Carrie and Endicott are having an affair, but the build-up of circumstantial evidence over the past five months could convince even the most skeptical observer—as it has finally convinced him. The first signs came early in the friendship, when he became aware that the gravitational pull that brought the foursome together was between Carrie and Endicott.

Other signs emerged one at a time in the following weeks. There'd been a marked change in her sexual behavior, for instance. Carrie now goes to great lengths to avoid situations that typically lead to sex with George. She persists in this until she can't avoid it, at which point she allows him to climb aboard and root around on her and in her until he has his orgasm. During this activity she is uncharacteristically passive. Thereafter, she manages to avoid sexual encounters with him for another couple of weeks. Occasionally she even resorts to "I'm just too tired." Which they both know is nonsense, because she's a whirlwind of energy in every one of her activities. In fact, she fills her life with furious busyness that includes more-or-less continuous renovation of the house, restructuring of flower beds, photography (boxes of photos and framing materials fill an extra bedroom), bicycling, skiing, hiking, and running. He worries about the running. Before Endicott, she ran at noon, or after coming home from work. Not now. Her early morning runs with Endicott are an hour of adultery opportunity four or five days a week and she's been doing it for months.

George thinks about the last time she's *not* been too busy or too tired, and concludes it was the evening two weeks ago when he returned from New York and trapped her, in a weak moment, apparently, into consenting, and got her half way up the stairs before Endicott showed up on the porch, with Susan in tow, apparently as cover for his visit to George's wife.

It occurs to George that at night Endicott gets Susan and in the morning he gets Carrie. Shit, he's fucking *both* of them, and I'm not fucking either one. He feels deserted *and* deprived.

This makes him think of his worst moment. It came on the third or fourth time the two couples had shared dinner. The four of them were standing in the kitchen drinking wine and chatting while George cooked. George had turned away from the range and took up his glass just in time to catch the moment when Endicott raised a bottle of wine and looked at Carrie. She'd smiled and said, "I need food first—I get way too loose when I drink on an empty stomach." Endicott had looked at her like only she and he were in the room, and said, "What's wrong with that? You should try it." Carrie had been smiling and watching him pour the wine, but when she heard his words, and the tone of his voice, her smile faded and she looked intently up at him and held his gaze for several seconds.

That duration of the encounter was small, but the intensity of the encounter was not: for Carrie and Endicott, in that moment, no one was in the kitchen but them. George had glanced at Susan to see if she also witnessed the exchange, and she had. The moment passed, but the character of that evening, and of those that followed, changed.

The dinners became regular events, with frequent touching between Endicott and Carrie. Often they managed to position themselves together, and when they did, leaned a bit toward one another, as if one was the negative and the other the positive of two poles of electrical force. Inevitably, conversations involving all four of them drifted into communication between Carrie and Endicott.

Over the months George often objected to the frequency of their shared dinners, but immediately relented when Carrie pushed back. He never articulated his misgivings. In fact, he is now thinking uneasily, he has simply gone along with her wishes, to avoid conflict. He wonders if this has given Carrie permission, but rejects the idea as foolish.

George is startled by the ring of the telephone. He picks up the handset and hears a feminine voice: "Hello George, I hope you don't mind me calling you at work."

The voice is familiar. "It's okay," he says, and waits to hear the voice identify itself.

"It's Susan," the voice says.

"Oh, hello Susan. How are you?"

"I'm okay. How you doing?"

"Fine." She pauses. "Actually, I'm not fine. There's something I need to talk to you about."

Of course George knows what that something is. As the force field around Carrie and Endicott identified them more and more as a couple he and Susan have passed many glances, but he has avoided talking to her about his concerns. "Oh?" he says reluctantly. "What is it?"

"I'd rather not talk about it on the telephone. Can we meet?"

"Sure."

"Are you free this afternoon? It's kind of personal. I'd like to talk about it privately. Could we meet at your house or mine?"

It suddenly occurs to George that she may know something he should know. He decides he wants this meeting, but he wants it in his territory. "How about our house?" he says.

"Okay."

℘

George stands at the French doors watching rain pound the deck. The gusting winds of the morning are gone, and now the rain has come, and it comes straight down, drumming the roof, rattling the skylights, hissing on the deck and the hot tub cover. The cumulative effect is a dull, distant roar.

The doorbell chimes and George turns and goes into the hall. She stands under the porch roof, the sky black behind her. Her hair is wet and clinging, making her eyes look big and childish.

"Come in, come in."

"That was so stupid," she says. "It wasn't raining, so I walked out of the house without even an umbrella. God, look at me."

She shrugs out of her jacket and stands helplessly holding the sodden thing.

"Here," he says, "let me take it. There's a towel in the bathroom."

She goes into the hall bathroom. When she comes into the kitchen he is draping the coat over a chair back. She speaks through the towel, which is flopping around her head. "What an idiot." She lowers the towel and combs her fingers through her hair.

"You must be cold. I'll find you one of Carrie's blouses."

"That'd be great," she says.

He fetches one of Carrie's sweat shirts, which she takes back into the bathroom.

When she comes out he says, "I'm making tea."

"That sounds good."

The activity of organizing the tea kettle and the cups and the teapot occupy him and allow him to think about her errand. "You wanted to talk." he says.

"Can I have a glass of wine first?"

"You don't want tea?"

"I'm so nervous. It's wine I really want."

He gets a bottle of wine from the rack. "Sure. Red okay?"

"Red's fine."

He pulls the cork and pours two glasses. She takes one and drains half its contents. He waits until she lowers her glass, refills it, then takes up the other glass. The tea kettle begins whistling. He turns the burner off and the whistling subsides.

"I've never gotten a read on you," she says. "I never feel like I know what you're thinking." She raises the refilled glass and sips, then moves to the French doors. "I don't think you read me either. I guess it's to be expected—Carrie and Endicott are so lit up with one another they've blinded both of us. When I step back and look at the thing, we just seem to be following along, like a couple of suitcases. It's too weird for me."

"Yeah. I know."

"My mom told me not to do it," she says, looking out at the rain pounding down on the hot tub cover.

George guesses: "Marry Endicott?"

"'He's in a different place in life. He's too old for you. He will lose interest in you after the novelty of having a young woman wears off.'" With an ironic half smile, Susan looks back at George, who stands leaning against the island. "It appears she was right."

"It would seem so." George says, because he thinks she expects him to agree. He moves up beside her at the French doors.

She raises her glass and sips. "He's very competitive, very controlling. That was what Mom saw." She looks quietly at the rain and the black sky. "There's something I have wanted to ask you. I have seen you—sometimes—*looking* at me." She glances sidelong at him. "Like I said, I don't get a read on you. Maybe I'm wrong."

George gets it, finally. He makes his calculations and decides. "No, you are not wrong. I *have* looked at you— often—and I suppose you've sensed—that—that I want you."

She sucks her breath, as if this is a shocking revelation. He knows it is not; he simply gave her the answer she has set up with her question. He wonders: did Carrie approach Endicott as directly and did he respond as directly? George knows that would be Endicott's style.

In the silence that follows George's words she looks down at her glass and swirls the wine, as if waiting. Finally, she looks up at him with a smile. "I think you're supposed to do something now. It's your move."

He has been a faithful husband for twenty years, but, prompted thus, he finds it easy to say what this neighbor woman requires: "Let's make love."

"Okay," she says with a softer smile, "but can we do a tub first? To put us is in the mood?"

"Yeah, sure." He opens both sides of the French doors and stands for a moment watching the rain.

"We've never done a tub in the rain, have we?" she says.

He thinks of the times the four of them have donned bathing suits after dinner and sat in the tub and drunk Cointreau or Drambuie or port. "No, we haven't. I think it's time."

"I want snow," she says irrelevantly.

George faces her and takes her wine glass and places it, with his, on the counter. "Okay, anything you want. After we get in the tub."

She laughs and watches him unbutton his shirt, and responds by gracefully peeling Carrie's sweatshirt up over her head and pushing her jeans and panties down until she can step clear. She steps into the rain and he follows. He folds the cover off the hot tub. Tendrils of fog rise into the rain. George watches her climb into the tub and sink neck-deep in the steaming water. He climbs in and stands looking down at her face, noting that her cheeks are pink.

"Let's do it here," she murmurs.

ϾϿ

Water vapor rises like fog from her gleaming skin as she stands. She lifts herself up onto the wall of the hot tub, and with her legs dangling in the warm water, takes up her wine glass. "I feel so good," she murmurs. The rain has tapered off to a fine mist that settles out of the clouds like a fog. She arches her back, raises her arms, and closes her eyes.

George sits neck-deep, his legs outstretched. He is looking into the shadows between her legs, which, seeing the direction of his gaze, she obligingly reveals more fully.

"Is it easier now?" she asks lazily, cocking her head.

He doesn't understand.

"The score's even," she amplifies, "which softens the pain. But I have to admit I feel pretty strange. Sort of detached, like I'm too numbed to know what I feel."

"If it was a four-way game the score would be tied at one-one-one-one," he says, attempting to match her tone. "We're gonna have to do this again or we're gonna fall behind."

"You want more? Already? You came twice."

He smiles. "I'm thinking medium term here, not near term."

"This evening, after I tell Endicott that I've been fucking you, I'll leave him. After that, we'll see. Maybe I'll want to do you again."

"Was that why you fucked me? So you could tell him you fucked me?"

"Of course. And it *does* help. Don't you think?" She sips her wine and studies his face. "Or does that kind of talk hurt your feelings?"

It does hurt his feelings, but he says, "No."

"But I don't want to talk about that; I want to talk about revenge. I can get behind that without feeling anything more than what I feel right now. *You* should tell her first. It has to come from you."

"I kind of like you telling Endicott and Endicott telling her. It fits with your revenge model. If I tell her it becomes a confrontation between her and me. The message will be more disturbing to their relationship if it comes from you to him, then to her."

Susan thinks about this. "Yes," she nods. "Yes, you're right. This will make them unhappy together. Maybe it will even break their concentration on one another. Yes, I like it. Besides, Endicott hates to lose, and this way I get to tell him, "You lose, sucker." He'll need some Tums before I leave." She smiles and sips her wine. "You get it that they think we're stupid, don't you. That, compared to their fucking, we're unimportant."

He realizes that he no longer has an appetite for this conversation or for Susan. He has discovered what there is to discover and is disappointed. The hot tub and the exertions of sex have made him tired, and now Susan makes him tired. Her brittle, writerly wordplay no longer amuses. *She* wants to hurt Endicott and Carrie. *He* wants Carrie separated from Endicott and back in his life, just like it was the day before Endicott and Susan moved into the house down the block. His regrets are different from hers, as are his motivations: right now, at this moment, he wants to preserve and she wants to destroy.

"How long have you been married to Carrie?"

"Twenty years. Most of the time it was good."

"I've had five with Endicott, and after the first year it wasn't much fun most of the time. He's very self-centered, as if you haven't already noticed, so the only time I was happy was when I wanted what he wanted. I've let him do some ugly things to me, but the worst thing, the absolute worst thing he ever did was seducing your wife while I watched you watching him do it. Isn't that *too weird*? It was like you were in on it." She raised her nearly empty wine glass and drained it. "But I tied the score, and I feel good about that. In fact, when you were inside me, I felt so good I began to believe I'm going out the winner."